A KILLER SHOT

A PARKER PHOTOGRAPHY COZY MYSTERY

PARKER PHOTOGRAPHY COZY MYSTERY SERIES

SUZANNE BOLDEN

LAUGHING DEER PRESS

CONTENTS

Our lovely sandy beach area on the Wisconsin River was not on a par with the Bahamas. But we loved it. And over this past summer, the Book Nook had a hard time keeping its so-called *Beach Reads* display fully stocked. Summer tourists, looking for a relaxing read while sunbathing or for passing time on the inevitable rainy or chilly days, quickly bought up the books. Ginger's years as a librarian served her well. Customers also appreciated her selection of jigsaw puzzles for the same reason, a relaxing vacation time activity. Ginger's new bookstore proved a resounding success and a great addition to Harmony.

In August, with the start of school, Ginger worked with the staff of our local schools to compile a curated list of reading material for the upcoming school year.

She donated copies of those books to the school library and made them available in her store. She often ran specials, especially in popular series. Mothers and grandmothers alike loved all the children's books she carried.

My book, *The Harmony Apparel Collection,* was prominently displayed along with other books written about the Driftless area of Wisconsin. Creating that book was a labor of love for me. When Eleanor Harmony, the matriarch of our village's founding family, revealed the extensive and well-preserved clothing in her family's mansion, the Historical Society went to work creating an exhibit around them. Mandy, my soon to be daughter-in-law and I devoted hours to photographing the garments to include in a beautiful coffee table book.

Ginger shared the space with Grace and Dermot Murphy's coffee shop. This meant she had a constant flow of customers who wandered over to browse as they sipped on their coffee. Her welcoming sofas and easy chairs encouraged them to sit and rest for a while.

Now, this early September air had hints of the coming fall in it. I was looking forward to the cooler weather when she would light the fireplace discovered buried behind the walls of a previous remodeling.

Ginger was holding a special author book signing event today. Another wise marketing decision to bring people to her shop. This event featured the recent memoir of a professional golfer. She did it to coincide with a professional-amateur tournament being held tomorrow at the Driftless Golf Course. Through the front windows I could see she and the author were arranging his display table, getting ready to open her doors in a few minutes.

I savored the fresh brewed coffee odor that hit me when I pushed open the door to Murphy's Coffee Shop and Bakery. The aromas of baked goods made my mouth water. I smelled a hint of pumpkin spice scent. Fall was in the air! The coffee shop seemed especially busy this morning. I had to wait in line for my coffee.

"And will you be having your usual maple frosted donut with that, Jackie?" Grace asked as she poured my coffee.

"No, I think I'll try whatever Dermot baked that has that delicious pumpkin smell."

"You won't regret it. It's yummy. By the looks of this morning crowd, he'll be busy all day. Would you like the pumpkin spice muffin or a donut?"

"I'll take the muffin. Are these people here waiting for Ginger to open up?"

"I'd like to think they are here because of our pumpkin spice specials, but truth be told, you are probably right. Ginger should open the French doors between our places any minute now," Grace said as she plated my muffin, added a napkin and fork, and handed it to me. "Will you be buying Mr. Moreno's book?"

"I might get one for Scott. I know he'd enjoy it. But I'll get out of your way here now. Dermot's playing in the golf tournament tomorrow, right?"

Grace nodded as she took the order from the person behind me. I slipped outside to find a seat, even though the air held a fall morning chill. A signboard announcing the book signing event included the best-seller lists *My Life on the Tour* appeared on, along with accolades from other well-known golfers. My photographer's eye appreciated the well-done publicity photo of Carl Moreno, a suntanned, confident looking man.

I watched as Stu, our own local newspaper reporter, editor, and publisher, strolled toward me from his office just a couple of doors away.

"Waiting to get one of Carl Moreno's books signed?" he asked with a wink.

"I might. Scott would enjoy it." I patted the chair next to me. "Can I buy you a coffee?"

"You know, I will take you up on that. Carl Moreno provided me with a publicity release for the print paper, but I wanted to ask a couple more questions and take some photos for our online edition." He looked at his watch and took a seat. "Guess I'm a little early."

Returning with Stu's coffee, I said, "I'm glad I finally get to treat you. I've enjoyed so many cups in your office."

"That you have," Stu chuckled. "And I enjoyed every minute of our conversations."

"Even when I asked you to investigate things?"

"Especially those times." Stu rolled his shoulders back. "Investigative reporting is still in my blood."

"And Harmony is lucky to have you. Are you playing in the tournament?"

"Yes ma'am, I sure am."

After a few minutes of chatting, we saw Ginger open the Book Nook's front door. "Looks like she'll get a great deal of business with this author," Stu remarked.

"And Grace's coffee shop too," I said, noting that most of the people inside the coffee shop moved through to the book side when Ginger opened the interior doors. "Are you going to play a practice round today?"

"That was on my mind. I've played some this summer but sure could use loosening up for tomorrow. My darling Kim has a way of talking me into taking on situations which I wouldn't choose on my own. But now I find I'm getting rather excited. I'm looking forward to seeing who my partner will be. Maybe he'll be one of the professional golfers I've seen on television. Hope he's patient with my play," Stu said.

"Or she," I said, knowing there were four women professionals registered to play tomorrow too.

I wish I had time today to practice, I thought. My golf game improved since Scott and I started playing at the beginning of summer, but I was still clearly an amateur. How did I get talked into playing in this tournament? Junene! She, along with other seasonal residents of The Hills Resort, wanted to give back to the community and have fun with it. They came up with this golf tournament idea, and the beneficiary would be the Harmony Museum and Nature Center.

It was called a pro-am tournament, which meant they partnered professionals with amateurs. The amateurs were notable locals, community members, and political figures gathered from Harmony, Greensville, and even from Madison. Our pros were a mixed bunch, including some who no longer played professionally, and some who were golf course pros from the surrounding area.

"You'll have to wait until tomorrow morning to see who your partner is, Stu. Junene thought it would be fun to announce pairings the day of the tournament. Unusual, but that's Junene."

"She did a great job of bringing them in early," Stu

said. "Many of the golfers arrived yesterday to relax and enjoy themselves in our beautiful corner of Wisconsin. Travis had all the boat rentals out for today and the fishing guides were busy this morning."

While Stu chatted, I noticed that many of the faces of those entering the bookstore were not familiar to me. By their looks, they must be some of the pros. Excitement was certainly building. I found myself impressed with how well Harmony was handling the growing number of tourists. I knew my photography business was going gangbusters since I moved back and, with help from Todd and Mandy, the online sales were a big part of it.

"Why the big smile, my dear Jackie?" Stu said.

"I was just thinking about how well our residents were handling all the busy tourist times. Remember all the noise made when the golf course was being prepared?"

"Yes, I do. People were concerned about the beauty of our famous hills being stripped away as they carved the golf course out. The protestors by the front gate caused a stir. And of course, the murder of Rick Ballard, the construction supervisor, didn't help quiet things down."

The memories flooded back to me. "And then that awful incident involving Alan Morris' body. I was out there that day with Dave and his drone when we managed to stop Alan's body from being buried by an earth-moving machine." I shivered.

"And on what eventually would become the thirteenth hole. Spooky, if you believe in that sort of thing. Wasn't he connected to Eleanor Harmony's fiancé? The guy killed in that car crash?" Stu's brows pinched together. "He was a partner of his, maybe?"

"He was."

"Didn't you and Patti trick the killer and prove he did it?"

"We did. Excellent memory, Stu. We lured Winford into a trap out at Patti's family farm."

"Good thing you moved back to Harmony, Jackie. Where would we be without our amateur sleuth? Say, Kim told me you and Scott are planning your wedding at the Harmony House. Is that true?"

"Yes, it is. Your invitation to the reception will be in the mail soon. We're not planning on a big shindig, but we want to celebrate with close friends."

"That whole red dress thing with Kim and Luella Hagge at the Harmony mansion was another mystery you solved. They just keep popping into my head."

"Kim has been a help with the murder investigations too, don't forget," I said.

"Yes, she has. Sometimes I think inserting herself

into investigations isn't smart, but like I said, she has a mind of her own. And Kim is excited you'll be remodeling and adding more gallery space at Parker Photography. Guess that coincides with you wanting to move out to Scott's," Stu said with his cute little grin.

"Scott and I have been completing plans for redoing my apartment to become part of the studio and gallery."

"So, will you be moving to his place before the wedding?" Stu said with a wink.

"Nope. The move into Scott's home will wait until after the wedding. You won't believe how many times I've been asked that very question."

Stu stood to leave, but not before teasing me. "Well, it is hard to believe there are still traditional gals left! I'm heading inside to get a few photographs and some quotes. See you tomorrow."

CHAPTER TWO

The signing line inside the Book Nook was moving slowly, so I got a refill of coffee and returned to my outdoor seat, warmed by the sun. My mind drifted to ideas I was considering for the studio remodeling. Looking at the Parker Photography storefront from this angle gave me the opportunity to picture what would catch the eye of someone on the square or walking on Main Street. How could that cute second-floor balcony off of my apartment turn into an appealing and useful element of the gallery? I knew it must remain because it brought me joy over these past months. Just ornamental? No, it should have a purpose. Perhaps a place for customers to relax? Would I be offering wine or coffee and teas inside and they could take them out on it at a little bistro table? I liked that idea.

Kay Whitlow, owner of the Whitlow Bed and Breakfast, exited the bookstore and stopped at my table. "I popped in to see how my guest was managing. I pictured Carl sitting alone at his author table with no one showing up to get an autographed book. But I was sorely mistaken. It's packed in there!"

"He's staying with you?"

"Along with several other golfers. Luckily, he brought extra books to sign. Good thing because Ginger said it's been a record day of sales. Not only of Carl's book, but other popular golf books she brought in for the weekend."

"I'm getting an autographed copy of *My Life on the Tour* for Scott. I was just hovering out here enjoying the day and waiting for things to slow down."

"You'd better not wait too long, Jackie." Kay rolled her wrist to glance at her watch. "I've gotta run up to Harmony House to make sure things are getting set up for tonight's event."

"Are you still covering the treasurer's duties while Trudy's away helping her father?"

"I am. There's added pressure with that as well. I'll watch for you golfing tomorrow. Hope you get one of the young, handsome pros."

"Haha! No more looking for me. I've got my own handsome man waiting in the wings. But I'd like to play with someone who can give me some golfing tips."

Thinking Kay might be right about the books running out, I went inside. Ginger was lifting another stack of books and putting them on the table where Carl Moreno sat. He nodded his appreciation even as he kept talking with Kim Walters, Stu's wife. I overheard her ask him to sign the third book for her cousin Bert. "He's such a huge fan of yours, Mr. Moreno."

"You can call me Carl," he replied. "There now. Thank you for all the purchases you made. I hope the lucky recipients enjoy your gifts."

"They will. I just know it. I hope my husband Stu gets you as a partner tomorrow. He would be thrilled. Course that other golfer from, hmm, where did Stu say that was? The tall, lanky guy. Usually wears green on the last day of the tournament. I can't think of his name, but Stu said he'd like to play with him. No offense to you, Mr. Moreno." Kim paused and notched her shoulders up with a coy grin. "I mean Carl. I'm sure he'd be just fine to partner with you as well."

Ginger discreetly steered Kim away from more conversation with Carl, so she wouldn't further tie up his time. She pointed her in my direction. I hurried toward the register to purchase my book for Carl to sign, but Kim followed.

"Ginger said you had something you wanted to ask me," Kim said. Over her shoulder I saw Ginger do a palm up so-sorry gesture.

"Ah, hmm. Oh yeah. I was going to tease you about not wearing a red dress to the event tonight. I don't need a flashback." Thank goodness I'd just talked with Stu about past events. The one with Kim falling down the Harmony mansion's main staircase in her red gown popped into my head at just the right moment.

"Oh, goodness no. This isn't a formal dress code, is it? Gosh, did I miss that?"

I'd begun to say no, but Kim kept up her side of the conversation before I could get the word out.

"I thought I'd wear a cute new suede jacket I just bought in Greensville. It's such a stunning shade of that perfect fall rust color." She flipped her long hair behind her shoulder.

"Bet it will look good with your chestnut-colored hair."

"Why thank you. So do I. I'm thinking about my camel-colored trousers and a hunter green sweater. It should be a fun night. I heard they have lots of silent auction things. Did you donate something?"

"Yes, I did. In fact, I have to run it up to the…"

"I knew you would. You're such a good citizen. Stu and I put together a basket with a year free subscription to the Harmony Happenings and a free home value estimate from me. It's hard in real estate to come up with things to offer, so I'm including cute mugs with golf sayings on them. I heard Hannah and Mark have an antique mirror in a gilt frame. I may have to bid on that!"

"Kim, if you'll excuse me, I'm going to have the author sign a book for Scott. It looks like Carl's time here is ending in a few minutes."

Kim brushed aside my remark. "Don't worry about that. I bet he'll stay as long as there are people waiting. But I need to go. See you at the event tonight at the Harmony House later. Tata."

I got in line to wait for my turn. There were only three people still waiting.

The woman in front of me turned to look back. "Getting that for yourself?"

"No, I decided my fiancé would enjoy it. There certainly is a great deal of interest in Mr. Moreno's book. Are you in town for the tournament?"

"I'm playing in it. Angie Palmer. No relation to Arnold," she said with a shrug. "Wish I had his skill, though."

"Jackie Parker. Nice to meet you. Are you here as an amateur?"

"No, believe it or not, I'm here as a professional. My pro career has waned," she said. "I've gotten into a couple of senior tours, but my days as a top-notch golfer are over. But it's always fun to do charitable events like this."

"That's very generous of you. Have you played our course before?"

"I haven't, but I've heard good things and I'm looking forward to it. Are you playing tomorrow?" Angie asked.

"I am. I'm hoping I don't make a fool of myself, but hey, like you said, it's for a good cause."

Her turn came up, and it became obvious that she and Carl knew each other when he stood and gave her a hug.

"Angie! Is that really you? What a delightful surprise."

"Hi Carl. I was so excited for you when I heard about your book. Congratulations. It'll be fun reading it and learning all the buried secrets of the tour. Am I mentioned in it?"

Carl opened the cover of his book and tapped his finger on the acknowledgements. "Right here. You were one of my inspirations. I always admired the way you approached the mental game. It really made an impression on me."

I saw the emotion on Angie's face. She clutched her autographed book to her chest. "You can't know how much that means to me. I'll see you on the course tomorrow. Thank you!"

Carl waved me up to his table. "Hello, thank you for purchasing my book." He opened the cover and looked up expectantly.

"Please autograph it to Scott. He's my fiancé and has taken on the challenge of making me into a presentable golfer."

Carl smiled up at me. "How's he doing?"

"It's a work in progress."

"Say, you look familiar. Is there somewhere we might have met? Wait. Hold on. I know. I saw your head shot just this morning. Up at the place I'm staying. You're a professional photographer, right?"

"Whitlow's B&B? Yes, Kay is a friend and generously allows me to display my photographs."

"They are lovely. You live here in Harmony?"

"I do. I have a gallery here. And I'm one of the area amateurs playing in the tournament tomorrow."

Grace stepped up to Carl's table with a fresh cup of coffee for him. "She's a celebrity to us, though. World-famous photographer. Here you go, Carl. Looks like you're finishing up here. Stop over at Murphy's for a cookie or cupcake on me. My husband Dermot once saw you playing at a tournament at Whistling Straits. He'd be honored to meet you."

"The Straits are one of America's most beautiful links courses. Do I detect an Irish accent coming from you."

"You are right. We immigrated to America from Ireland."

"Your country has some of my favorite courses. I'd be happy to join Dermot for a coffee and one of those delicious pumpkin spice baked goods I've been smelling all day."

CHAPTER THREE

The Harmony Mansion had once belonged to Gustave Harmony, founder of the local paper mill. Eleanor Harmony, devastated by the death of her fiancé on the eve of their wedding, donated it, along with surrounding grounds, to our Harmony Historical Society. When Eleanor subsequently married her fourth husband, the longtime family groundskeeper, they moved into the modest home her family first owned upon arriving here in Wisconsin.

Driving up the winding road toward the mansion, Scott and I enjoyed remembering the events held here when we were children. The Harmony family had generously opened their home to school children. Pony and hay wagon rides, along with tours of the milking parlor and plant nursery, were part of our childhood.

Now that it was open to the public and available for events, I was proud to be a member of the committee making the museum and nature center an important part of the community. But thinking about the times spent here working on *The Harmony Apparel Collection*, and remembering the red dress mix-up episode, was looking backwards. Tonight was about the future.

The golf cart paths and walking trails were constantly being expanded. They now linked the course, the resort, the Harmony Museum, and the village green together. This meet and greet event for the golfers and locals was highly anticipated, and it looked like lots of guests took advantage of the paths as there were dozens of golf carts in the parking area.

The key drivers of the tournament idea were a group of women who lived part time at the Hills Resort surrounding the golf course. They'd taken to calling themselves the Real Housewives of the Hills, a parody on the television series. I was sure they'd all be here tonight, and I looked forward to congratulating them on their efforts.

Large baskets of fall mums lined the edges of the walkway and the porch steps. The vivid orange, bronze, yellow, purple, and red flowers greeted us as we entered the mansion.

"Jackie! Scott! So glad you made it." Kay was on the

front steps greeting guests. As head of the Historical Society, she was, in essence, the hostess tonight.

"We wouldn't have missed it. I can't believe how stunning the house looks," Scott said.

"And these grounds! You all have worked wonders here since you took it over." I was so proud of my friend. Also a transplant from a big city, she became a successful small business owner and an active member of our community.

"Thanks so much. I appreciate that. But Junene and her group were instrumental in making tonight happen. I'm looking forward to the funds this tournament will raise. It should top off our roof replacement account. Go around to the back. Jeff is on the patio. Glad we pulled out the heat lamps. Looks like temps will be dropping. I'll catch you later."

We made our way on the flagstone path to the back of the house. Scott reminded me of the time he held the ladder as I climbed the large trellis here, looking for evidence in the infamous red dress case. "You were sure determined to get up there. I admired such spunk from an elderly woman," he teased.

"And to think I trusted such an old man to hold my ladder?"

We found our Chief of Police and Kay's boyfriend Jeff talking with a man he introduced as Fred Foster, mayor of Foster Town. "Fred here was telling me about him being on the tour years ago."

Fred smiled. "Ah yes, that was long ago. But I was grateful to be invited to this event to relive some of my small past glories. I'm not sure yet if I'm here as a pro or an amateur. The invite came to Mayor Fred Foster, so I'm guessing it's as an amateur."

"Nonsense," I said. "I'll bet you're one of the pros. Were you on the tour together with Carl Moreno?"

Fred cleared his throat. "Yes, well, you might be right. Now, if you'll excuse me, I'm going inside to bid on some of the silent auction items. I'll see you all tomorrow."

Through the atrium windows, I saw Angie, the golfer I'd met at the bookstore. She was chatting with Dorothy, my Aunt Ruth's friend from Shady Pines. I decided to step inside to join them and hoped Dorothy knew where Aunt Ruth was.

"Jackie, look who I just found. Angie Palmer! I can't believe it!"

Angie looked in my direction and smiled. "I'm more recognizable than I thought."

"Are you a golfer, Dorothy?" I asked.

"I was. Loved the game. But few women players of my generation ever made it as far as this woman."

"Angie and I met at the bookstore today. Carl

Moreno even put her name in the dedication of his memoir," I said.

"That overwhelmed me. Carl is a true gentleman and a terrific representative of the sport. But nice as it was to see his familiar face here, it's such fun meeting fans of the game like you, Dorothy," Angie said.

"Nice to see you again, Angie. Dorothy, I was looking for Aunt Ruth. Have you seen her?"

"She was by the silent auction tables inside," Dorothy said.

I made my way through the atrium and into the parlor, where I found Aunt Ruth chatting up the guests to bid on the auction items. The entire picture reminded me of when I met Scott as he bid on auction items from the fundraiser that ended with the murder of Luella Hagge, wearing the identical red dress Kim had worn. Boy oh boy, the ghosts of evenings past were in full mode today.

"Looks like you are turning huckster for the evening," I said to Ruth, who was busy talking up the silent auction items to anyone within hearing range.

"Jackie! Am I glad to see you! You picked the perfect photograph of the Driftless course to donate. It's going for well over your original asking price. The celebrity golfers here love it." She scooted down the line and held up the bid sheet for me to see. "Just look at this, already over a dozen bids."

"That's great."

"And the Driftless's donation of gift certificates to the pro shop and the course were so generous. I'm amazed at how well this is going! Monday we'll be busy counting receipts."

"Don't they get split with the winner of the tournament's charity of choice?" I asked.

"No, that's a separate thing, involving registration fees. Is Scott here with you?"

"He's outside. I just wanted to let you know I'll be seeing you at the Wednesday potluck this month. Sorry I missed the August one."

"That was your trip to California, right? And you didn't even find a wedding outfit in Los Angeles after going all the way out there. Such a shame."

"But it was worth the trip to see Alli and Beverly. Did I tell you they are going to be here for the wedding?"

"No, you didn't. I'll bet you're happy about that. You mentioned wanting to look again at some designs in the Harmony collection. Why not tonight? We could slip away for a few minutes."

Before I could answer, Kim came bounding up. "Isn't this grand? The Antique Market and the Taste of Harmony food festival put Harmony on the map, but now we are on an even bigger map! Ginger just told me she had her best day ever at her bookstore. I think I'll be helping her hunt for a new home soon. Murph seems ready to pop the question any day now. Have you met Carl Moreno, the author?"

"I met him at the Book Nook earlier. Remember? We talked to each other too."

"Oh, gosh, you're right. I can be so spacey." Kim did a spin around, waiting for a compliment on the outfit she'd told me about.

"That looks great on you, Kim," I said, elbowing Ruth.

"Ah yes. Lovely as ever," Ruth said. "I'm glad for Ginger. She's a smart businesswoman. Oh look! Rocco has arrived. If you two will excuse me, I'm going to suggest a few things he might want to bid on."

Kim stretched her neck and stood up on her toes. "I've lost my Stu again. Have you seen him, Jackie?"

"I think I saw him with Senator Bennett a minute ago. That way."

I pointed in the general direction of the front hall and, with Kim distracted, I slipped away to the portable bar set up in the atrium. The special they were offering was an Arnold Palmer.

"That sounds great. I hope it's the spiked version."

"I'll make that happen, ma'am," the bartender said as

he reached for a bottle of vodka and added it to the lemonade and iced tea.

Now back out to the patio, where Carl Moreno had joined Jeff and Scott.

"Jackie, nice to see you again," he said. "Harmony throws a great welcome party. I will give them that."

"I see you've met my fiancé, Scott, and our chief of police, Jeff."

Carl turned to Scott. "You're a lucky guy."

"That I am. And Jackie's starting to enjoy golf too. We plan on traveling around the states together, checking out courses."

"Sounds like an excellent plan. Wisconsin has some terrific golf courses. And I'm excited to play the Driftless. I've heard good things about it. I took a tour of your lovely hills and checked out the course this afternoon. The views of the river and the surrounding hills and forests are striking. Nature always takes my breath away, no matter how old I am."

"I thought you were signing books today," Scott said.

"This was after I was finished at the bookstore. Speaking of that, here comes the owner," Carl said.

"Hey boss, wasn't expecting you at this bash," Murph said to Jeff as he and Ginger walked up.

Ginger took Murph's arm and said, "Carl, this is my

boyfriend, Patrick Murphy, also known as Murph. He works in our police force."

"Nice to meet you, young man. I spent a good amount of time with your special gal today. She's not only a lovely lady, but a hard-working one too."

"I wanted to thank you again for arranging your book signing to coincide with the golf tournament. For a small-town bookstore, this was a windfall day," Ginger said.

"My pleasure," Carl said. "You were an excellent hostess. I'm going to make the rounds to say hello to some buddies I haven't seen in a while. Enjoy your evening."

"Nice guy," Jeff said as he turned to Murph. "All set for tomorrow?"

Murph nodded. "Golfers aren't known for getting rowdy and the fans will be spread out along the course. I think it should be an easy day."

"And how's the issue with the shooters in the hills?"

Ginger shot Jeff a stunned look. "What shooters? And in what hills?"

"Just young men target shooting. But with the cooler weather, the mosquitos are gone, and I think they show up more frequently," Jeff said with a laugh. "No worries, it's not some militia group forming."

Murph hitched up his belt and put his arm around Ginger. "I'll protect you from those outlaws, honey."

"Cameras set up?" Jeff asked.

"Yes sir. Motion activated ones. The images come to my phone so I can move them on along if they show up tomorrow."

"Is this special for the tournament?" I asked.

Jeff shook his head. "No, not really. Just needed doing. Besides, if we can avoid random gunshots ringing out while the world, or at least our local channel viewers, are watching, it would look better for us. The television station will broadcast live, won't it?"

"Sure will," I said. "I'm going to check out something upstairs. Want to come with me, Scott?"

With an obvious twinkle in his eye, Scott put his arm around me. "What is it you want to check out? If there's any way I can help…."

I leaned against him and looked lovingly into his eyes. "Dresses from long ago."

He pulled away. "Ah, I'm okay here with Jeff. Look, there's Ruth. Maybe she'll go with you."

Ginger chuckled and shook her head. "Men. I'd love to go with you, Jackie."

I hooked my elbow into Ginger's. "And I'd love you to come along."

After picking up Ruth along the way, the three of us

headed to the front hall. We climbed the grand staircase in the front hall up to the second floor.

"I've poured over your book's photos, but to be here and actually touch the garments!" Ginger stopped. "Though I probably shouldn't be touching them."

"I won't tell," I said.

Ruth ran her finger over her lips. "Neither will I."

We conspiratorially moved toward the wing where the garment display was housed, along with other historical pieces, such as photographs and possessions of the Harmony family.

Passing by the balcony, a tense exchange of words rose from below.

I stopped to listen.

CHAPTER FOUR

"You got a few facts wrong, old buddy."

"Really. Like what?"

"Don't play innocent. We both know what happened. Only I got the raw end of the deal."

"Don't threaten me."

"Threats go both ways."

"Threat. That's a strange word coming from you."

Then a third person entered the conversation. I peered over the railing but couldn't see who the first two men talking were as they stood close against the staircase wall.

But the third man walking toward them was Senator Robert Bennett, and he said, "I'm surprised you'd show your face here with your legal difficulties."

One of the men replied, "I'll straighten those out."

Then the senator remarked, "Just a warning. You're playing with the big boys now."

That was a strange exchange. I wanted to hear more, but Ruth and Ginger had already entered one of the display rooms. I hurried to catch up to them.

I wasn't sure about just why I wanted to see the garments again with fresh eyes. When I couldn't decide on a wedding gown in California, nor in Milwaukee or Chicago, I felt stuck. What did I want? What was missing in the hundreds of ideas presented to me at viewings, from magazines, or well-meaning friends' texts? Never having dwelt on being a bride, this felt off kilter. I remember teenage friends who dreamed of that special day. Down to the details of what they were wearing.

"Are you hoping something here will inspire you, Jackie?" Ginger asked as she ran her hand over the velvet bow on the back of a silk taffeta evening gown.

"Yes, and I just got inspiration! Velvet. I want to incorporate the touchable warmth of velvet. The depth and richness of a deep color like that bow attract me."

"But don't you want to wear white?" Ruth asked.

"Maybe a cream color, but not some white flouncy puffy gown. And remember it'll be during winter, so practically I'll want something warmer."

"Just wear a nice coat," Ruth said. "Once you're inside the house here, the weather won't matter."

Ginger said, "Where's that velvet coat you photographed for your book? It really caught my eye."

I remembered most all the items on display because I'd photographed them for the book, but I couldn't remember a velvet coat. Maybe Mandy took those pictures because I was training her at the time.

"I know which one you mean. It's displayed right here." Ruth led us toward another of the bedrooms.

"That's the one," Ginger said. Her hands now clasped over her heart. "It's even more beautiful than the photograph."

The stunning evening coat hung on the shoulders of the mannequin. A rich navy velvet, full-length, white ermine fur trimmed evening coat. I gasped out loud. "That's it. That's just what I want!"

But Ruth stood there looking genuinely confused. "A navy coat?"

"No, probably not navy. It's the design of this coat I like. The clean white trim against the soft velvet. I love it! What about red velvet for the Christmas season?" I asked. "And then underneath, a simple long gown in a… oh I don't know what sort of fabric for the dress. But I have to have a coat like this for my winter wedding day."

"Well then, that's settled. You should have it custom

made, Jackie. Do you know anyone who does that anymore?" Ginger asked.

Ruth rubbed her chin, her brows furrowed in concentration. "Whew, that's a tough one. But I'm sure we'll figure it out. This style it is. If we find someone to make it for you, maybe she can work out a dress design, too. We only have a few months to go. But for now, I'd better get back to the party. I told Rocco I wouldn't be long."

"Don't want him worrying about you," Ginger teased. "Thanks for letting me join you up here. Would you like me to order you a new bride book? They have the most amazing planning guides. From the save-the-date to the bridal shower. All the steps lined out."

"Why don't you order it for yourself, dear?" Ruth grinned at Ginger. "I think Jackie is skipping a lot of the traditional bridal doings."

I knew what she meant by suggesting it for Ginger. "Ruth is right on both counts. I'm keeping it quite simple, but when I see the way Murph is around you, I think he's ready to pop the question."

Ginger's cheeks reddened. "Do you think so?"

"Take it from someone who's photographed many young couples. You two are perfect together. He's a keeper."

"Speaking of keepers, there's Rocco now," I said. He

stood at the base of the grand staircase, talking with Fred Foster. What a classically handsome man Rocco was. So confident and at ease, yet he held an inner strength built up in his years of being an investigator with federal agencies. And he was a terrific dresser on top of that all.

We interrupted their conversation, but Fred excused himself, saying he had a long drive ahead of him and he needed to be fresh for tomorrow's golf.

"Jacqueline, I understand you are planning a reception here in December," Rocco said. "If I may be so bold, I hope to receive an invitation."

"I thought my aunt might invite you as her guest," I said with a wink. "How's that sound, Aunt Ruth? Will he be your escort, or should I send his invitation separately?"

Rocco took Ruth's hand in his and raised it to his lips. "Please grant me the honor of being your escort for the nuptials of your niece."

Now it was Ruth's turn to blush. "Of course, you will be my escort, silly man."

CHAPTER FIVE

This was by far the busiest I'd ever seen our golf course. Cars prowled the parking lot, looking for a space. An announcement blasted out over loudspeakers letting everyone know there was a continental breakfast being served. I made my way to the enormous white tent that dominated the lawns near the clubhouse. A local car dealer parked a shiny red SUV outside the entrance to the tent as an offering for a hole-in-one. But I passed by it, focused on finding the registration table.

"Pairs were drawn earlier, and you're with Carl Moreno. Your team goes out second," Junene said as she saw me coming toward her. "Lucky you!"

"That's great. He's so nice. Maybe I'll get some tips from him. Who's Scott going out with?"

Junene ran her finger down the sheet. "Angie Palmer. They go out toward the end of our lineup."

Olivia interrupted us. "Junene, they're looking for you at the clubhouse. I'll take over here."

"Sure. I've checked Jackie in already. We have about half of the golfers registered. Catch you later, Jackie."

They placed the names and photographs of all the golfers on a large board and added the scores as they came in. Sponsors were featured for contests ranging from longest drive to closest to the pin. Nearby was a television crew with our local sports reporter interviewing Carl Moreno and Angie Palmer. A small crowd had gathered to watch.

I found Scott hitting at the golf simulator toward the back of the tent. Jeff and Kay watched and teased him about saving all his strength for the game coming up. I slipped in next to them.

"Who'd you get partnered up with?" I asked Jeff.

"The golf pro from a course down in Milwaukee. Seems like a nice guy. We go out toward the middle of the players, so I won't tee off for a while. How about you?"

"I'm with Carl and Scott's with Angie. The ones getting interviewed."

"My dad used to watch him years ago," Jeff said. "I'm not familiar with the woman golfer."

"The networks rarely televised the women's tournaments back then. Dorothy knew of her and is going to make sure that her beer cart pulls up where Angie's playing."

"The Shady Pines gals are the beer cart girls? Too funny," Kay said.

"I know. They will be a hoot."

"Scott's really improved his game this summer. Did you teach him a few things?"

"Yeah right." I laughed.

A voice over the loudspeaker announced that the first four pairs should make their way to the tee box.

Carl took my elbow. "It thrilled me to see we'd be partnered up, Jackie. I think we have a most excellent chance of winning. Don't you?"

"Except maybe by my sweetie and his partner," I said.

Angie nudged Scott. "If only I was a couple decades younger, I'd give you a run for your money, Jackie, and not just on the golf course."

I took Carl's arm. "The gauntlet has been thrown. May the best golf team win!"

Scott gave me a quick kiss. "Watch your back. You may come in early with good scores, but Angie and I are second to the last and we'll know just how much to kick it up to beat you two."

. . .

I couldn't have believed how nervous I felt walking up onto the green. I'd never had such a large audience watching. The television sports announcer was there to introduce each pair of professional and amateur golfers.

"Ladies and gentlemen, please welcome Jacqueline Parker, world famous photographer and owner of the Parker Photography Studio and Gallery. The Parker family has been a part of this community for over sixty years. And I think I see Ruth Parker, one of the original owners, driving one of the beer carts today." A laugh rolled out across the course as Aunt Ruth waved from her gaily decorated cart.

"Jackie is paired with professional golfer Carl Moreno. A Wisconsin native, Carl has won two major opens. He is also a best-selling author, bringing autographed copies of his book, *My Life on the Tour*, to Harmony's new bookstore and one of the many sponsors of this tournament, the Book Nook. Please be sure to check it out after the tournament."

An even louder cheer rose for Carl as he walked up to me. He took my hand and raised it up in the air with his. Then with a bow, he swept his hand toward the tee box and said, "Ladies first."

I didn't whiff the ball. I hit it straight. My nerves settled.

Carl teed off and our caddies, high school golf team members from the surrounding area, picked up our bags and we were off!

Once we were in the game, the day seemed to fly by. Carl was a fun golf partner, sharing stories of his time playing professionally and what he called tales from the road. He gave me tips only when I asked. Before I knew it we were on the eighteenth tee and our round ended. Since we were the second team out, much of the audience was still walking the course following favorite teams.

We agreed that a cold beer would taste great. Carl was delighted to see Sally Collin's cheese curd wagon, and he started to make a beeline for it, but stopped. Carl looked at his phone before he spoke. "Good news and bad news. I have to run some more autographed books down to the Book Nook. I have them in my trunk, so it shouldn't take too long." He handed his unopened beer to Junene, who had joined us, and with a chuckle said, "Hold my beer, dear. I'll be right back." He walked a few steps, then turned back to add, "Eh, go ahead and drink it. Enjoy!"

More teams came in, but as I looked at the leader board, we were still on top. Surprisingly, the Senator's team was next highest. Mayor Fred and Doc Potter were pulling up the rear as they approached the thirteenth hole.

I joined some of the other golfers who'd also finished. Charlie Hunt and Orin from the Stone Mill were among them. We all agreed on how well the course played today. Deciding I needed a bathroom break, I headed for the course's clubhouse, where the golfers had privileges, when I sensed an unease move through the crowd.

When I was leaving the clubhouse, Junene skidded up in her golf cart. "Jackie, come with me. Hurry."

I'd barely made it in the cart when I heard an ambulance siren coming up the hill. Junene raced along the cart path, shouting out broken sentences to tell me what we were headed toward.

CHAPTER SIX

"*A* shooting?"

"Yes, one golfer is down on the thirteenth hole." Junene leaned into a turn, and I grabbed the handle on the dash.

"Serious condition?"

"That's all I know. Scott called me saying he heard the shot, followed by a shout from the team behind him. He kept me on the line as he raced over to where the players were. I heard him say Fred is down and Doc is kneeling next to him. Then he hung up, and I called for the ambulance. I need to get out there and see how bad things are."

As we raced across the course, all the spectators and golfers turned with questioning expressions.

"I'll bet it was those kids Murph's been trying to oust

from the woods in the hills above the course. They target shoot up there. And Lord knows what else. The resort residents have been very unhappy about it, but it's on private land, we're told."

I can't believe this. We were almost there, and I prayed that Mayor Fred was okay. It was a good thing Doc was there for him. Junene got another call. She pulled her phone out and handed it to me as she continued her race to the thirteenth hole.

It was Scott. "Jackie, where's Junene?"

"She's right here with me, Scott. We're on our way there. Is Fred okay?"

"Doc said he seems stable, but there might be internal injuries and bleeding."

"Tell him the ambulance was just arriving and should be right behind us somewhere," Junene said.

I relayed that information to Scott, and I heard him tell Doc.

"Okay. Thanks Jackie. Tell Junene I'm calling Murph. The shot came from the direction of the hills behind the green. He should get there right away."

As we moved closer to the hole, I could see the audience nervously milling around. The volunteer golf course marshals were keeping them back away from Doc, who was still bent over tending to Fred Foster.

"How's he doing?" Junene asked Doc before she even got off her cart.

"Hard to tell, but he's stabilized and speaking. I'm trying to keep him calm, letting him know that we've got him covered and will be taking him to the hospital."

Fred, extending his arm, reached up. Doc leaned closer to hear him.

"What's he saying?" Junene anxiously hovered over Doc.

"He asked what hit him. I said a bullet, probably from someone's target shooting. He made a joke saying that he was a better golfer than they were at aiming at targets."

I breathed a sigh of relief. If Fred could kid around, it meant that he was okay. It was good that he maintained consciousness too.

The ambulance arrived shortly after we did and took over the treatment from Doc, who insisted on riding along to the hospital. When they got Fred on the stretcher, he gave a thumbs up signal to the crowd, and they raised a cheer.

CHAPTER SEVEN

"What a crazy thing to have happen," Junene said as we made our way back to the clubhouse. She contacted staff and instructed them to spread the word that Fred Foster was wounded. But he was alert and told us all to go on with the tournament.

"He might just have been in shock," she said. "But what can we do? We might as well go ahead. We can ask everyone to say a prayer for him later at the awards ceremony."

Before we left to return to the clubhouse, Junene convinced Scott and Angie, who balked at returning to their game, that it was for the best. A text came in from Doc and Junene had read it out loud.

"Fred expects to win a prize at the ceremony. I assured

him you'd come up with something. Doc's text ended with a smiley face and thumbs up. So please, let's all go on as though this didn't happen. Now I'm heading back to find that prize that Fred's looking for. See you back at the tent."

As the wind pushed against me on our drive back, I couldn't help but think she was right. What would shutting everything down achieve? At least the teams could complete their rounds and the prizes be handed out at the end.

"If those target shooters caused this, I'll ring their necks. Jeff simply must put a stop to it." Junene's white-knuckled fingers looked like she was taking it out on the golf cart's steering wheel. She flexed her hands to get the blood flowing.

"Murph said they had agreed to not practice today. And there's only so much the police can do. They are on private land," I said.

Junene abruptly stopped the golf cart and looked at me. "Baloney! There's got to be a law protecting innocent golfers from having bullets whizzing by while they are playing. There has to be a nuisance clause or endangerment. This can't go on this way. One of my neighbors is afraid her pet could get hit with a stray bullet. We love being here where it's quiet and safe. We never expected to be living in the Wild Wild Midwest!" Then she hit the pedal and with a jerk, we rode the rest of the way to the clubhouse in silence.

This was troubling. Junene was right. Whoever fired that shot had to be brought up on some sort of charge. Maybe Murph would find some evidence on his motion detector camera. Thank goodness Fred seemed to be okay. Then it hit me. That could have been Scott whisked away in the ambulance. Or Angie. They'd just played that hole. I gasped when I realized I'd just stood on the very spot where the body of Alan Morris was found.

Was the thirteenth hole haunted?

Everyone welcomed Junene's assurances that Fred wanted us all to play on, and the subdued atmosphere loosened up in the big tent.

When the last team came in, everyone let out an enormous cheer. The tops were pulled off the chafing dishes to reveal hamburgers, pulled pork, and grilled brats accompanied by colorful peppers and roasted onions. Fresh corn on the cob was next to bacon topped baked beans. Trays of fresh fruit and vegetables added pops of colors. Orin's Stone Mill Brewery employees operated beer kegs while the local 4-H club members offered cold sodas and water to the golfers and their guests.

Scott and I sat with Angie and Carl, who'd returned

from his book run to the Book Nook. He was shocked to hear what had happened to Mayor Fred. "That's insane. Who heard of such a thing? I target shoot. I hunt. In fact, I'm leaving town tomorrow and heading out to Montana for a scheduled hunt. But I've never been careless with my firearms. My prayers go out to Mayor Fred that he will fully recover."

Angie said, "When you miss the target, the bullet goes somewhere, doesn't it? Could it possibly have traveled out across the course?"

"Sure," Scott said. "But targets have back stops and are usually positioned where bullets can't stray into public areas."

"Will the resort see that charges are filed against the shooter?" Carl asked.

"I certainly hope so, if Murph can find them," I said. "I know that Junene won't rest until he does."

"I don't blame her," Angie said. "This puts a cloud over the event. I will watch for an email update letting me know how Fred is and who was to blame for this most unfortunate accident. Is this range you're talking about an official licensed one?"

"No, it's not. These are young adults, who hang out there in the woods and plink around, as they call it..."

"Doesn't the owner kick them out?" Carl asked.

"Apparently not. Maybe after this he will. I think he's

an uncle of one of them. This isn't the first time that corner of our hills was used by kids. It was a notorious party place when we were young. Hidden away on a back road."

Between bites of his hamburger, Scott mumbled. "Good parking spot, if you know what I mean."

Angie and Carl burst out laughing. "I haven't heard that word in a long time. What about you, Angie?"

Her shocked expression didn't fool anyone. "How could you even suggest I would know such a thing, Carl Moreno?"

Junene was attending to Master of Ceremony duties up in front of the room. She caught our attention when we heard Angie's name.

"We'd like to hear a few words from one of our celebrities, Angie Palmer. Let's give her a round of applause."

Angie stood to speak to those gathered here. "Thank you! I'm honored to be part of this event. The Wisconsin golf community is growing every year. I was sorry to hear Steve Stricker was not available to play today. He missed a fun event on a beautiful course. And so did Mayor Fred Foster. His round ended at that old bad luck thirteenth hole. I know we are all praying for his continued healing. We know his love of golf is as strong as ever. And so is his sense of humor. He directed Doc to send a text that he expects to win at least one prize given out here today."

The crowd burst into laughter and cheers.

"And now back to Junene to present the winners."

Junene stepped back up to the microphone to announce the trophies and prizes.

The television reporter approached our table. "Mr. Drake and Ms. Palmer, you were playing in front of the victim, one Fred Foster, correct?" he said. "Did you hear the shot? Did you see anything unusual?"

"We heard the shot but have no further comment other than that he was alert and talking when he left. Of course you should keep his name out of the news until next of kin has been notified. Now if you'll excuse us, please." Scott handled the awkward moment politely, but firmly.

CHAPTER EIGHT

Scott let out an enormous sigh when he saw Stu approaching. "I hope he's not coming here as a reporter, but as a fellow golfer."

"Hey everyone. Quite a day, wasn't it?"

"How'd you shoot, Stu?" I asked.

Stu pointed to the scoreboard. "That says it all. Not last, but far from your first-place position, Jackie and Carl. Congratulations!"

"Thank you, sir. But now if you'll excuse me, I believe I'll return to my room for a nice hot shower," Carl said as he pushed back from the table.

Angie joined him in excusing herself. "I too would like to get out of these clothes and clean up."

Stu saw his opening. "Scott, I didn't want to ask in

front of them, but what's your sense of what happened out there? You can tell me honestly what you think. I won't publish it. Off the record. But I'm asking this as a concerned citizen. Are we safe in Harmony or is there a mad gunman on the loose?"

Scott rubbed his temples and glanced in my direction before he spoke. "Honestly Stu, my best guess is that this was a terrible once in a lifetime accident."

"Kim had a big commercial property showing in Greensville and had to leave before the shooting happened. I'm so glad she wasn't here. She'd be absolutely distraught to know a golfer had been shot. Have you heard anymore from Jeff?"

"We haven't. He's having his officers search in the hills. But it's such a broad area. Murph has a line on the kids, young adults who target shoot up there. But with this recent bullet going far astray, something will have to change," I said.

"When I moved here, I never expected the population growth we've seen," Stu said. "It has affected our quiet little village in unforeseen ways."

"This certainly caught everyone by surprise," Scott said. "I just hope and pray that Fred comes through it."

"I'll have to address this in Tuesday's edition. By then, I should be able to get a comment from Fred.

Hopefully, I'll be able to share the news that he's back home and on the mend."

"Stu, are you going to add information to the online edition?" I asked.

"I almost have to, don't I? But what? I don't want to bother the family, but I do owe it to our community to report events. Maybe I'll call Jeff later and see what his opinion is about it. I noticed the local news reporter talked with you, Scott. Did you tell him anything I could use?"

"Nope, just that Fred, the victim, was awake and speaking."

Stu nodded. "I understand. I'll be able to reassure Kim things are okay. You know how she can get worked up."

As I walked Scott to his pickup, Aunt Ruth and the Shady Pines gals waved as they drove away in Dorothy's car. I knew Harry and Elmer had been somewhere on the grounds watching the tournament. On a whim I'd also bought one of Carl's books for the library at Shady Pines. I was sure they'd enjoy it.

Almost everyone had left, and I decided to see if Junene needed help to close things up. Junene certainly never expected anything like this to happen today. I thought she handled it masterfully, and I wanted to let her know that.

I found her on her cell phone in a corner of the big tent with a piece of paper dangling between her fingers. Hanging up, she pinched her face into a perplexed look and slowly shook her head before saying, "What can I do for you, Jackie?"

"Just wanted to see if there was anything I could help you with here."

She looked slowly around the area as if coming back to reality. "Let me think. The tent company is coming tomorrow. Looks like the young people we hired for cleanup are starting now that the guests are gone. I think things are on track on my end."

"Some of us are meeting at the Wildwood Supper Club tonight. Would you like to join us?"

"I appreciate that, but I have loose ends to clean up before I head home and put my feet up to think about what happened out on the thirteenth hole today. Can you believe it? I guess we will now be perceived as the Wild Wild Midwest like I said before. Won't we?"

Should I laugh or not? I didn't know how to take her comment.

"It's okay. Laugh. It was a joke. But if the law catches those target shooters, they should charge them with something. Maybe reckless endangerment. I don't know the legal terms, but dang, something has to put a stop to such careless use of firearms."

"You're right, and I know Jeff is fired up about this, too," I said.

"This is one of my loose ends." Junene held up the paper. "I've been trying to reach Fred Foster's emergency contact, his wife. I've left several messages asking her to call me back. But I haven't gotten a response yet."

"Maybe she's in the hospital with him and can't talk in his room."

"I suppose you could be right. The hospital would have ways to notify next of kin."

"Why were you trying to reach her?"

"I wanted to apologize personally for what happened and see how he's doing."

"It's not your fault, Junene."

"I know that."

"Did you try his office?"

"The mayor's office in a town the size of his is basically nonexistent. It's his phone number personally and probably his office's too. So, no. I didn't try to find an office number."

"Maybe Jeff reached her. Did you ask him?"

"No, but that's a good idea."

"Better yet, he's supposed to meet Scott and I for supper at the Wildwood later tonight. How about I talk to him about you wanting to reach Mrs. Foster and see what he has to say? For now, check that off your to-do list."

"Thanks so much, Jackie. Now I'm one step closer to putting my feet up!" Junene stood to give me a quick hug as her cell phone rang and she walked away.

CHAPTER NINE

It surprised me to see Carl had joined Kay at the Wildwood.

"I'm not making a move on the police chief's girlfriend," Carl assured me with a chuckle.

"Glad you could join us to celebrate your win." Scott clapped Carl on the shoulder. "Jeff's not able to make it, Kay?"

"He's running late, so we decided to have a drink here at the bar first," Kay said. "And yes, let's make this a celebration for Jackie and Carl. Top golf team!"

"I heard you were in town. Big shot author now. It crushed me when you didn't show up here to say hi," Lynn, the Wildwood's head bartender, said as we settled into our barstools.

"I made plans to be here tonight, Lynn. Just to see

you! But when Kay kindly suggested I join her, it sounded better than drinking alone."

"You know each other?" I asked.

Lynn was a local celebrity in her own right. She'd been here at the Wildwood for years, and much like Dolly at the diner, knew most everyone and what they'd order.

"Know him? Who doesn't? He's famous!"

"Not hardly," Carl said, shaking his head with an embarrassed grin.

"Well, you are," Lynn proclaimed. "Years ago, Carl's caddy was from Harmony, and he'd always bring him here for a celebratory dinner when they'd get back from a tour. Nicest famous person I know."

"As soon as we were near Harmony and Lynn's old-fashioneds, my mouth would start watering. And I would not have left town without one this trip either."

As Lynn set our drinks down, she brought up the shooting at the tournament today. "Were you all there when that shot was fired on the course today? I couldn't believe it when I heard about it. Is the guy okay?"

"I was playing right ahead of him," Scott said. "Haven't heard any more about how he's doing, though."

I felt too exhausted to think about it. I tried shifting the conversation away from the shooting by asking Lynn what tonight's specials were. Lynn was reciting them to us when Jeff arrived, still in his golf clothes. He had little to add on Mayor Fred's condition, but said he would interview him in the morning and would let us know.

"Interview him about what? What would he know about kids' target shooting in the woods?" Scott asked. "From everything I've heard, this was an open and shut case."

Jeff didn't answer the question but instead reached for the drink Lynn handed him. Scott repeated himself.

Jeff took a sip and set his drink down. He clasped his hands around the glass, staring at the glistening ice cubes as though they held the answer. "I think I need to consider the possibility it wasn't them. Those kids or some strangers using the targets set up in the woods."

"Are you kidding, man? Why?"

"Do you know something we don't?"

"Seriously, what else could it be?"

The questions from all of us flew at Jeff. Kay protectively tucked her hand into the bend of his elbow.

He looked up at us with tired eyes. "Hold on. Let me explain. I haven't been able to reach Fred's wife, and according to someone in the nurses' station, neither has the hospital. He's not improving. I finally found someone who updated me. They're operating tonight to stop internal bleeding."

This is where I brought up my talk with Junene this afternoon, explaining she'd been trying to reach her too. "I told her I'd be talking to you tonight and let her know if you reached next of kin."

"I spoke to her, Jackie. The county sheriff who covers the town provided me with some phone numbers of people who might know where the mayor's wife is. That's about as far as I've gotten. Decided I needed some nourishment."

"Has the news broadcast information on the victim of the shooting yet? Don't they wait until next of kin are notified?" Kay made a good point.

"That's usually the way it's handled. They've called me and I know the hospital received calls as well. We've not told anyone who it was. I hope the reporters respect the family. This could be totally innocent, but I'm becoming concerned that we might be overlooking something by assuming it was those kids. Murph reached the landowner, and he assured him that the young men who use his land would be at the police station in the morning."

"Wow, that's horrible. Poor Fred. To be all alone and facing surgery. I wish there was some way I could help find next of kin. Isn't he mayor of a tiny town full of Fosters?" Carl asked.

"He is. It's basically a four-way stop size town. Feed

store, a tavern, beauty salon, auto repair, and a dollar store. From what the sheriff told me, there are only a few of the original Fosters left. I talked to a distant step-cousin who couldn't help and a great-aunt in her nineties who I couldn't make heads or tails out of. Neither knew where Mrs. Foster was and when they asked why, I didn't provide any detail, only giving them my phone number. But now that his condition is getting more serious…I'm not sure how much I should divulge to them."

Our dinner conversation was much lighter. Carl talked about how he was looking forward to his Montana hunting trip. Kay hoped to get the financial things wrapped up in the morning and then present them to the committee, who would meet in the late afternoon. She quickly accepted my offer of help as she was pulling double duty.

"Sure you're not up for the treasurer's position?" Kay asked. "Pretty please? They would easily vote you in."

The thought of helping her with it tempted me, but no way was I going to commit to anything more to do this fall. Between the wedding planning, finalizing plans for the new space, and running my current business, I had enough on my to-do list. I gave her an emphatic no. "But I have a suggestion for you. Would Harry take it on? He strikes me as a numbers kind of guy."

"Not a bad idea. I'll ask him about it. He's always seemed to want to be in the background, though."

"Wouldn't hurt to ask and it might flatter him," I said.

That night I left the windows open to get the cooling night air. I fell asleep thinking about my good luck with Ruth showing me the velvet evening coat. Now to find a dressmaker. If only I had access to the costumers that Alli used in her film. I needed to find a talented seamstress in the area.

But once asleep, my dreams took me elsewhere, disturbing my night's rest.

CHAPTER TEN

haking off my morning drearies was easier once I remembered I'd be going to the Harmony Museum to meet up with Kay this morning. I'd check out that evening coat again and see if I got that same giddy sense of perfection I'd had on Saturday night. I should take more photographs of the details. Ooh…maybe I could try it on!

The parking lot was almost empty. Tourists were few and far between this time of year, but once the fall colors came out, they'd be back. Entering through the front door, I headed up the grand staircase to the Historical Society offices. Voices came from the second floor. That must mean more of the committee were here to help Kay.

"Morning, Jackie," Kay greeted me.

With Kay were Aunt Ruth, Eunice, and Betty from Shady Pines. "What a pleasant surprise! What are you guys doing here?"

"This one said we should show up or shut up. So I showed up 'cause you know I can't shut up," Eunice grumbled.

Ruth's exasperated sigh caught my attention. Were the girls having a tiff? "That's not at all what I said."

"Ruth's right," Betty added. "Eunice, you're just being an old sourpuss."

Kay shrugged her shoulders and grimaced.

"Eunice, what's bothering you?" I asked.

"Your aunt told us that you're fiddle-faddling around about what dress to wear to your wedding. I was just sharing my opinion on it with her. She didn't appreciate it and said I should tell you myself. Geez, it was no big deal."

"You made me uncomfortable," Betty said.

"That's easy to do," Eunice mumbled.

Betty asserted herself. "You should not be allowed to just spew things like that out to us. Now tell her directly what you said." Betty fidgeted under Eunice's glare. "Please."

Eunice curled her lips and let out a low growl.

Out of the corner of my eye, I saw Ruth stifling a laugh. What was going on here?

"The rest of it now," Betty said.

"Oh, good grief. I said it was a waste of time worrying about. Just get a nice dress."

Ruth said, "And…"

"Now you're making me feel like an ignorant, nasty old lady. But Jackie, Scott will be much more interested in what you wear to the marriage bed than what you wear to the ceremony."

After getting over my laughing fit, I took Eunice's wrinkled face in my hands. "I can assure you, my friend, I've had that nighttime apparel neatly tucked away for weeks.

"And Betty, I thought you'd be conditioned to where this one's mind and mouth take her, but please don't worry. I take no offense to what she said."

Eunice wiggled her finger at Betty, who responded by sticking out her tongue and bursting into laughter. "We had you going, didn't we?"

Ruth joked. "You were so serious when you said that. Look at us old ones trying to tell Jackie's generation what to do. Candidly I don't know that she sleeps on the couch when the weather, or the late hours, or car trouble, or whatever excuse she gives herself to stay overnight at Scott's happens."

"Ruth! Please, some decorum," I scolded.

Kay stood. "Alright, already. I've got to get to work

and since you four showed up, not much has gotten done. Let's get it on. Many hands make light work. Junene will come over shortly with some final numbers." She began delegating the duties in her usual efficient way and we all set about getting things done.

As we catalogued the silent auction pieces and the winning bidders, Kay worked on the expense billings from the welcome party on Saturday night.

Since they now all knew the story of the coat, but not what it looked like, I wondered if it would be okay if I went and tried it on. The old saying, better to ask forgiveness than permission, flitted through my mind. I walked out into the hall and down to the room to where the coat was on exhibit.

I ran my hands over the velvet. Do they even make fine fabric like this anymore? I sure hoped so. I released the hidden clasps and pulled it from the mannequin. Slipping it over my shoulders, I discovered it was a perfect fit. If I found a dressmaker, she could pattern it right off of this piece. Just change up the color.

Standing in the doorway, no one noticed me. I cleared my throat and struck a pose. When heads turned, oohs and aahs followed.

"That style fits you perfectly Jackie!" Betty said. "You'll look like a Christmas princess. You're planning on doing it in red velvet, though. Right?"

I did a slow turn. "That's the plan. What do you think, Eunice?"

"Looks like it would make a nice bathrobe," she snarked.

"It's beautiful on you," Aunt Ruth said. "You'll have to get the Kramer's horse and carriage to bring you up to the mansion. Like a scene from Dr. Zhivago."

Kay hadn't spoken. Maybe she didn't like that I'd taken it off the mannequin but didn't want to be a spoilsport.

"Kay? A penny for your thoughts."

"I'm speechless! It's stunning on you, Jackie. And it will delight the Harmony women from the past that you chose their design to reproduce," Kay said.

"What a sweet thought. It makes me smile even thinking of that. They were so stylish and fashionable. I hope I can find not only a talented seamstress but also one with an eye for design."

"Just like your mother," Aunt Ruth said.

My heart skipped a beat. She was right. My mother was also a fashion icon in Harmony. She didn't have the luxury of limitless funds to spend on clothing like the Harmony women, but she owned Vogue on Main and enjoyed purchasing garments at a wholesale price for herself. The shop was her passion, and it was the go-to place for the latest styles. But it eventually closed, like many small-town clothing stores. Big stores, like Marshall Fields, pulled local women away to Madison and Milwaukee to shop. Even though she had loyal customers, she just couldn't compete.

"Oh, my goodness! Ruth, what about that friend of Rocco's who just bought a cottage? She might be perfect!" Betty was bouncing in her seat. "You know who I mean. This is serendipitous. Absolutely magical!"

"Who's that?" Kay asked.

"Sonja. She moved in last week. Isn't she like a seamstress or designer, Ruth?"

Ruth's fingertips tapped against her cheek. "You know, Betty, you might be right. I'm not sure if she still does that or has any of her sewing machines and equipment with her, but yes, Rocco said something along those lines. That she was looking for a getaway spot to retire to. I'll ask Rocco to introduce us. She's kind of kept to herself."

"Maybe you can find out more by the Wednesday Potluck. Will she be there?" I asked, excited by the prospect of finding someone with the skills to recreate this coat draped around my shoulders.

"Like I said, she's been keeping to herself, but I'll see what I can do," Ruth said.

CHAPTER ELEVEN

Junene's arrival with her paperwork helped us wrap up our Historical Society accounting. We'd be ready for the meeting later today. Everyone profusely thanked her for doing this fundraiser for our benefit. Kay had prepared a lovely thank-you card we all signed, a fresh arrangement of flowers gathered from the grounds, and a lifetime membership, including a pass for her and guest to any paid events the Harmony Museum and Nature Center might host.

"Oh my, this is so thoughtful. But I owe you too. By choosing you as the beneficiary, we drew even bigger crowds than expected! All in all, a plus for both of us." Junene glanced at her cell phone and excused herself to take a call. But she quickly peeked back around the corner and asked me to come with her.

"It's Chief Jeff. I asked if you could join in on listening to his latest update." We walked outside to a bench near the front porch, where she turned on her speakerphone.

"Thanks for waiting, Chief. Jackie and I are both here now. Go ahead."

"Is anyone else able to hear us?" Jeff's voice came over loud and clear.

"No. We're sitting outside and no one else is around," Junene answered.

"The situation has taken a terrible turn and I want to keep it quiet for as long as I can, though I'm afraid that others will talk to the press soon."

Junene's body jerked up. "What's happened, Jeff?"

"Mr. Foster died."

I gasped as Junene slumped, her hand dropping to her lap. I leaned forward to take the phone from her so we could hear what else Jeff wanted to tell us.

"It's Jackie. That's awful, Jeff. We're both shocked."

"Well, brace yourself because there's more. When I got to the hospital, I was told they did not show a patient with the name Fred Foster. I explained that I'm the Chief of Police in Harmony and an accidental shooting occurred in my jurisdiction yesterday. An ambulance picked him up from the golf course in Harmony and transported him to your hospital yesterday."

"So, he didn't show up as a patient because he'd already passed?" I asked.

"No Jackie, listen to this. The woman I was talking to realized that she'd spoken with me yesterday. She reamed me out, saying that we'd misidentified the man as Fred Foster and how things were really messed up by giving an incorrect name. Our patient with the gunshot wound was Earl Foster. Then she tells me he died from internal bleeding."

Junene looked at me in disbelief. Her mouth hung open and she couldn't speak.

Jeff's words came out of the phone. "Junene? Jackie? Are you still there? Why wasn't the right guy at the tournament? What the heck happened?"

"Hold on, Jeff." Junene jerked herself up. "Do not put this on me. I checked the man in Sunday morning. I'd never met Fred Foster. When we were looking for pros, his name came up. I don't even remember who suggested him. But he agreed to play and sent a photo in for our publicity. The guy I registered looked like him. Why would I think it was anyone else?"

"Didn't you check his ID?"

Junene's voice rose. "Seriously. Check ID? We're not

some beer bar. Why would I check ID? He took the name tag I gave him and put it on."

"Sit down, Junene. Let's hear Jeff out. How'd they realize who he was?" I asked.

"Simple. They found his driver's license in a zipper pocket in his golf pants."

Junene snorted. "So, who didn't do that on the fairway, huh?"

"Both of you. Stop. Mistakes happen. Did you ever get hold of Fred's wife, Jeff? Junene couldn't reach her."

"No. But the hospital staff reached Earl's wife last night, and she was by his side when he passed. I was told she wanted her privacy, but they would let her know the police were looking to talk to her." Jeff's word cut in and out. "I have to take this. It's her calling me now." And he hung up on us.

Junene's phone began ringing, and I handed it to her. She glanced at the screen and clicked the button to silence it.

"Aren't you going to answer?"

"I do not want to talk to some spammer now. What will happen, Jackie? Earl and Fred Foster deceived us. And now Earl is dead."

"It was a mix-up and an accident. I don't know why

Fred switched his cousin in to play. Or why Earl didn't say something that day. Maybe Fred just couldn't make it and didn't want to disappoint everyone. His cousin did alright. He was a high caliber player too."

The phone rang again. And again, Junene reached to silence it.

I stopped her. "Let me take it. It might be the hospital."

She pushed the phone toward me, and I accepted the call.

"Hi, this is Fred Foster. Is this Junene, the woman running the golf tournament?"

I explained who I was, and that Junene would be with him in just a second. I put Fred on hold and asked her if she wanted to take it. Her hand waved me off. I didn't want to hang up, so I asked, "Junene, please let me talk to him."

Junene's mouth opened, then snapped shut. She raised her eyes to look across the lawns. My guts told me that Fred needed to explain himself and I didn't want to let him go. "Maybe he can help us understand what happened."

With a deep, cleansing breath and a tiny nod from her, I took Fred's call. "I'm sorry, but Junene can't take your call right now. We just learned some dreadful news."

"That my cousin died?"

"Yes."

"Junene is angry at me for having him sub in, isn't she? I know she's right there with you. Can't she at least listen to my apology? Please put her on speakerphone."

I pushed the button and said, "Go ahead, she's listening."

"I'm so sorry, Junene. Please forgive me. I didn't mean to deceive you, but I fell ill Saturday night after the reception. Instead of canceling at the last minute, I asked my cousin, an avid golfer himself, to take my place. He was supposed to explain that at the registration table."

Unbelievable. I began to speak, but Junene took the phone from me and held it in her palm. "Well, Mayor Fred Foster, that didn't happen! We've been trying to reach your wife, thinking the injured man we sent off in the ambulance was you. You can certainly grasp our shock on hearing we had the wrong man."

"Yes, I can. But please take it easy on me. I just learned that I put my cousin in harm's way, and he died. Cut me some slack here. I never expected anything like this to happen."

But Junene didn't even pause to let that sink in. "Why didn't you call us immediately when the news about your cousin broke? You left us all looking like fools. And why didn't your wife return our calls?"

The tone of Fred's voice shifted. "Calm down. I told you I only learned this morning, and I called you just now."

Junene pushed back at him. "We've been waiting to notify next of kin. That would have been your wife, Mr. Foster. Our Chief of Police has been trying to contact Mrs. Foster. Where is she? Now Chief looks like an idiot because he's at the hospital and learns the man who just died is not you."

"My wife is bad with her phone, and she's been tending to our ailing aunt, so she probably just didn't turn it on."

Junene looked ready to burst. "That's no excuse in this day and age."

"The hospital found Earl's next of kin, didn't they? I don't know why your police department couldn't. Look. Let's both stop this. I don't want to argue with you. But if you can't be civil, I'll hang up."

Junene's jaw clenched, and she practically threw the phone at me. "You handle this."

"Mr. Foster, it's Jackie again. I'm so sorry you just learned about your cousin. We're dumbfounded that you only heard about this now. Didn't Earl's wife call you directly when she found out he was injured?"

"No, she didn't call me immediately. Carleen and I are not on the best of terms because of some, uh…family issues. I only learned at 2 o'clock this morning when Carleen called to tell me of his passing."

"And we just learned, too. This is a tragic situation all around," I said.

Fred continued. "I immediately called my wife Doris on our aunt's landline. The news hit her hard, probably because she's already stressed out about caring for a needy, elderly person. She checked her phone and told me about the messages Junene left for her. But she knew nothing about the event and thought it better I speak to Junene directly."

"As Junene said, our Chief of Police is at the hospital now and will want to talk with you. I suggest you call him immediately."

Fred didn't speak for a moment. "Um…sure. But why would he want to talk to me? Carleen said she was told this was an accident. Something about target shooting."

"The chief hasn't confirmed that part of this situation. It was the first thing he thought, but it's not conclusive that's what happened."

"But who would shoot at Earl?"

"The shooter might have thought it was you, Mr. Foster. Mistaken identity."

CHAPTER TWELVE

andy had the Tuesday edition of the Harmony Happenings newspaper spread open on the front counter. Her eyes remained glued to an article as she said, "Did you know Stu is asking that anyone with photographs or video footage taken near the thirteenth hole on Sunday to email him the digital version? This says he will work with the police in an effort to get information on the shooting."

I cleared my throat. "Good morning, Mandy. I'm fine. How are you?"

Mandy looked up with a grin. "Oops, sorry! Good morning, Jackie. I'm great."

"That's better." I teased her. It surprised me that Stu was having the photos emailed to him instead of the police department. Seemed like something someone familiar with the case should do.

"I'm going to go through the photos I took," Mandy said.

"Since I was playing, I really didn't take many, but I'll check them too. I suppose the news didn't make this edition. But have you heard that the man shot was not who we thought he was? He was a lookalike cousin to the pro who was supposed to be playing."

"What? That's crazy! Was this guy brought in as a ringer to win a prize? Bad luck for him. How is he doing?"

"I take it you didn't see the online news this morning," I said.

"With a little baby and a full-time job?" Mandy laughed as she went back to scanning the paper.

"He died yesterday."

Mandy's head popped up. "Oh, my gosh. I didn't know. And here I was being flippant. That's hard to hear. What does Jeff think happened?"

"Well, let's just say the double barrel whammy of news threw Jeff for a loop. Now he has an investigation with two possible victims."

"Someone else died?"

"No, but because none of us knew that Earl Foster was playing instead of his cousin Mayor Fred Foster, it could mean the shooter thought he was aiming at Fred. Or it could have been someone who knew Earl was the actual golfer, the substitute, and intended to kill him."

Mandy's eyes widened. "Whoa, that is complicated. But who would have known the golfer was Earl if he didn't tell anyone at the tournament?"

"His wife probably knew he was doing it," I said. "And Fred sure knew about the switch. No one running the tournament knew, but it could have been common knowledge back in Foster Town."

Mandy quickly put her hand over her mouth to swallow a snicker. "They have a town?"

"They named the place after their family. In fact, Fred is the mayor."

"Hmm…interesting. I'll start hunting through my photos. Though I don't know what I'm looking for."

"The shot that killed Earl came from the wooded hills at the edge of the course. Try to find photos from the thirteenth hole and leave the location data turned on. Did you take any videos?"

"I did a couple of you and Carl, and Scott and Angie playing. I know that Dave the Drone Dude took some, too. The course hired him to take video for future promotional use. I will let him know about all of this," Mandy said.

"Scott and Angie were playing right ahead of Earl

and Doc, so yours might contain something, too. I'm going over to get a donut and coffee. Want anything?"

"Nah, I had some donut holes Matt brought home last night."

On my way to Murphy's, I noticed Stu staring out the window of his Harmony Happenings office. Since the print edition was now delivered, he could take a little breather before beginning the update of the online news. Stuart Walters was once an investigative reporter who'd opted out of the hustle of the big city and bought the local newspaper, Harmony Happenings. He kept the paper edition, but added a daily digital news version as well. Some of the area residents only read the paper edition, but most were learning to check out the online version too. Especially if there was something where updates would be involved. Like a couple of weeks ago. Mrs. Krackhaus' Siamese cat pair went missing. These were her children and well-meaning neighbors and friends helped search. After the third day, she discovered them asleep on her front porch when she went out to get her newspaper, Stu kindly updated everyone online.

I decided to stop and talk with him, because I'm certain Stu would write an update in the online paper.

There was a little itch I wanted to scratch, too. Stu had good instincts, and I wanted to see what he thought about the Earl and Fred situation.

"Jackie, just the person I was hoping to see. I've had to eat my way through too many donuts because you haven't stopped to have coffee with me lately." Stu pulled a chair up to his desk and poured me a coffee.

"Morning Stu. How is Kim doing after the wild weekend?"

"She's settled down some."

"Smells like Murphy's coffee."

"You know it is. Theirs is the best!"

Stu put my favorite maple frosted donut and a napkin in front of me. "Stu, is my eating this donut the only reason you're glad to see me?"

Stu chuckled. "Ah, you know me too well. My dear sweet wife, in her own babbling, meandering way, shared some information she picked up Saturday night. She overheard a conversation between Mayor Foster and Senator Bennett. The Senator questioned how Fred's legal case was going. She asked if I knew what that meant, so I did a little research. The mayor is under indictment for mishandling government funds."

"Oh really? That's interesting, but surely you don't think he would have been killed over it."

Stu shrugged. "Who knows? I'm going to tell Jeff

about the conversation. Jeff can talk with Fred if he wants more information."

The clues were already coming in. Like this one. Put it together with the conversation I overheard on Saturday and who knows where it might take Jeff. Mayor Fred was a gambler and now might be a crooked politician too.

"Or do you think Kim should go talk to Jeff herself? I love her, but sometimes I know she inserts herself into the middle of situations when it might not be appreciated," Stu mused.

"Kim has helped expose criminals. She was critical in helping Jeff with the Langdon murders. And I was thinking about when she was in the sales office at the Hills Resort. She was a big help with those murders."

Stu squared his shoulders. "You are right. Kim was a part of that tangled mess with Rick Ballard and Alan Morris. I should trust her instincts in telling me about that."

"And let Jeff investigate if he wants," I said. But I could tell the investigator side of Stu was just getting started.

"Maybe it was a local from Foster Town who'd had enough of being cheated by the big family in town. So often the white-collar criminals get off. I could just be grasping at straws. Do you know any more about the case?" Stu said.

"I'm assuming you've heard that it wasn't Fred who was shot. Jeff talked with his wife at the hospital early yesterday morning."

"True, so the intended victim could have been Earl. But my gut tells me the person who fired the shot thought it was Fred on the course, and not his cousin."

"Remember, Jeff still hasn't ruled out an accident."

"Jeff let me know last night what I could publish, but it came too late for the print edition," Stu said. "Now I'm trying to compose a piece for the online paper."

"Oh, I almost forgot to tell you that Mandy is combing through the photographs she took and she's going to talk to Dave about his drone videos. Did you see the local news last night where one of their reporters got a statement from Earl's wife? She gave him quite an earful about that idyllic little town and her husband's cousin."

Stu's attention shifted from me to a point behind me. When I turned to look over my shoulder, my jaw dropped. We both stood and walked to the office window. There, on the village green of Harmony, stood a cameraman and reporter holding an NBC microphone up toward a woman with her back to us. Stu glanced up at the overhead television screen in the corner of his office. And when Stu reached for the remote and upped the volume, we heard what was being said.

CHAPTER THIRTEEN

"I'm here in the small quaint town of Harmony, Wisconsin, to interview the wife of Earl Foster. Mr. Foster, while playing in a charity golf pro-am tournament, was shot. We learned he passed away from his injuries on Monday. Mrs. Foster, what would you like the viewers to know about your deceased husband?"

The reporter extended his microphone toward Mrs. Foster, who reached out and grabbed at it. The reporter leaned precariously, but managed to hang on as she turned her eyes to look directly into the camera.

"My Earl was the sweetest man ever and would give the shirt off his back to anyone in need." With a choking sob, she dropped her head. The camera panned back to the reporter, who, with a gentle tug, regained control of the microphone.

"We can see that Mrs. Foster is overcome with grief."

But he was pulled out of frame when she once again seized control of the handheld mic. "He didn't deserve to die like this. Shot like some animal."

With a quick blurred movement, the camera refocused on them as the reporter asked, "Mrs. Foster, what are you hoping to accomplish by coming here to Harmony?"

"I must speak to the Chief of Police. I know he's already blaming some dumb kids' target shooting up in the woods. Says this is an accident. I can barely hold myself together. My Earl's body is lying on a cold slab in the county morgue and the police are not investigating who did this. They need to arrest the man who shot my Earl. Turn yourself in!"

The reporter held for the dramatic pause, then asked, "Do you know who might have wanted to harm him, Mrs. Foster?"

I watched the woman's eyes as they steeled, and she glared into the camera. "I do. For now, I will tell only the police. If they don't make an arrest this week, I will broadcast it to the world and all hell will break loose."

The reporter, left speechless for a heartbeat, responded. "Those are bold accusations, Mrs. Foster."

She spun toward him. "If you'd lost your life, your love, your partner in such a violent way, you too would say the same thing. I know they are saying this is mistaken identity, but that is…"

Not waiting for a swear word they couldn't bleep out on this live broadcast, the reporter spoke over Carleen Foster. "I would like to inform our viewers about the initial mix-up you are talking about." He turned toward the camera, signaling the cameraman to focus away from Mrs. Foster. But the camera stayed on both of them, and we watched Carleen's jaw clench and her nose twitch.

"Mr. Earl Foster had agreed to play as a substitute for his cousin, Mayor Fred Foster. The mayor reportedly took ill, and not wanting to disappoint attendees, arranged for his cousin to play."

Carleen leaned her face in toward the camera. Wild-eyed. "And Freddie knows what happened Sunday. He knows!"

"And now back to our studio." The reporter did a cut action across his throat to kill the camera. He leaned in, apparently to thank Carleen for the interview. She jerked her head up and jabbed her finger into the reporter's chest. We watched the reporter step back as she kept yelling at him, but we couldn't make out what she said.

With a huff, she turned and grabbed her large pink purse from the park bench and stomped away. Twisting her ankle, she quickly righted herself and headed directly toward the police station.

The small crowd that had gathered to watch the interview began to disperse, but one figure approached her. Kim.

Stu and I both spoke. "No!"

"What is she doing? That woman is out of control," I said.

We watched Kim reach out and touch the woman's arm, only to have her hand swatted away. But the forward bend of Kim's head meant she was persisting. This would not end well.

"I don't know, but she's not giving up and Mrs. Foster is no sweet church lady," Stu said. "I'd better hurry over."

"I'll come with you," I said, realizing Stu might need help to break Kim away from what she'd gotten herself into.

By the time we got to them, Carleen had gone inside the police station, leaving Kim ranting on the sidewalk. "The nerve of that woman. I was just here to offer my condolences, and she practically attacked me."

"She just lost her husband and is out of her mind with grief," Stu said, reaching to brush a stray hair from

Kim's face. "Don't let her upset you. By the way, is that the new outfit you were telling me about at breakfast? It's lovely on you."

A slight glimmer of pleasure passed over Kim's face.

"Stu's right. And those hoop earrings are the perfect complement to it." I grasped the distraction Stu provided.

"Aren't you sweet? Yes, this is the outfit. It's a little warm for today's mild weather though. But I couldn't resist. You know how much I love changing styles with the seasons. I appreciate you all trying to make me feel better. I shouldn't have bothered her. But I saw how upset she was. My heart hurt for her."

"You are a soft-hearted person, Kim. Where are you on your way to?"

Kim adjusted her scarf. "I need to talk with Patti at the Village Hall about a variance a client is requesting before they buy a property."

"How about I walk over there with you?" I offered.

"That's okay, but thanks. Did you hear what she said? She's trying to make our police, maybe our entire village, look like fools. Guns shooting off in the hills. Sloppy police work. Mistaken identity. We can't let that go unanswered. If she knows who did this, Jeff will get the person. He'll make an arrest and put the criminal away. This must be taken care of."

She paused. Then, with a bright light in her eyes, said, "Jackie, it might be up to you and me again."

Kim was getting wound up and heaven knows where she ends up when this happens.

"You were there that day. And you too, Stu! We must band together to hold Harmony's reputation as a safe and welcoming place. It's imperative for my career. And to the success of our small businesses. Like yours, Jackie. And Stu. All the love and care you've poured into keeping everyone informed with your Harmony Happenings."

"Darling, you're right, of course, but let's see what Jeff's interview leads him to do. We'll be at the ready to leap into action should he require help." Stu looked toward me. "Jackie, you and Jeff have a close relationship. He trusts you. Can you find out how the interview went and let us know?"

Just as I began to protest getting involved in this, Murph ushered Carleen outside. "Look, Mrs. Foster, I appreciate you wanting to share information, but Chief Jeff is currently with someone, and we can't have you making disruptions in our waiting area. If you'd like, my parents own a coffee shop right over there. And there is a bookstore next door to help pass the time until the Chief is available to talk."

Carleen's angry, impatient stare dared any of us to

remark on her circumstance. We all averted our eyes and let her walk off toward the coffee shop, hoping she'd calm down. Grace wouldn't do well with a customer outburst, especially one with a mouth like Carleen's.

CHAPTER FOURTEEN

With Kim off to the village hall, and Stu back to his office, I should make a move, one way or the other. Why was I hesitating? I had a reason to walk into the Book Nook. Maybe the book I'd ordered last week had arrived.

Jackie, don't put yourself in the middle of this. But the book might be there and I'm right here. I could grab it.

Jacqueline, stop. Turn right around. Go back to the studio. You have over eight portfolios to check out. You need to find the next photographer to display their work here. In a few months, the studio will double its usable space. Get going. A small shiver ran through me. And in a few months I would be married. Who'd have thought that would ever happen?

Jacqueline, I told myself yet again. Do not follow that woman.

I'm not really following her, my alter ego argued. It wasn't like me to let one angry woman divert me from doing what I wanted to do.

Carleen was at Grace's front counter, ordering coffee and pointing toward something in the bakery case. Good, she had calmed down. I walked into the Book Nook, where Ginger was helping a young man. "Be right with you, Jackie," she said over her shoulder.

Ginger had dismantled the big display of Carl Moreno's books and reduced it to a special display on a round oak table near the fireplace. I browsed through the new novel releases and found one in a mystery series I'd been reading, so I grabbed that.

Someone tapped me lightly on my shoulder, and I turned. It was Ginger. "Ready to help you. I assume you're here for that book you ordered." She reached behind the counter to retrieve it. "You're lucky. It was in a delivery late yesterday."

Her phone rang. "Hi honey. She is. Want to talk to her? It's Murph."

She handed the phone to me. It was Patrick Murphy. "Hi Murph, what's up?"

He first apologized for the interruption. Then said, "I don't know if you heard, but I directed Mrs. Foster to grab a coffee at Murphy's. I watched to make sure that's where she went. I saw you headed that way and took a chance. If you could hang around with her for just a while, make small talk or whatever, we'd appreciate it. Jeff wants to make sure she stays out of the way because we have Fred Foster in for his interview right now, and things might go south if they run into each other."

So that's why Murph practically pushed the woman out the front door of the police station. Here we go. How could I turn down the request? Easy, Jackie, just say no. But to be truthful, I'd already talked myself into following Carleen here. Now I was handed a reason.

"I suppose, but she saw me standing there with Kim. She'll suspect I'm up to something."

"You'll think of something. Please, Jackie. Jeff said we could count on you."

"He did, did he? Is it more than keeping her occupied? Cough it up, Murph. What else does he want me to accomplish? What is he counting on me to do?" I listened to what Murph had to say while Ginger rang me up. I racked my brain about how to approach Carleen. Entering the coffee shop through the interior doors of the bookstore, I saw her sitting at the small window table. Probably watching who would leave the police station. I picked up a coffee and headed to her.

"Mrs. Foster?"

"Yes."

"I wanted to apologize if Mrs. Walters bothered you out there. I watched your interview on television and I could see how difficult this has been for you."

"It was live? I didn't realize that. I thought they could edit it later. But don't matter, I said my peace. I didn't appreciate your Mrs. Walters getting all syrupy on me. I hate false words. Like I'm so sorry for your loss. She don't even know me or my husband."

"I didn't either." I indicated the empty chair next to her. "May I sit a moment? I just ordered this coffee when I saw you here."

She shrugged. Which was enough of an okay for me, and I sat down. "I was at the golf event. We were all in shock. And having listened to your interview, I must say I agree with you that it wasn't some hunting or target shooting accident."

She perked up. "You do. Well, good. I think you might be the first one who's told me that. That's all I've been hearing and reading. I know it's not true. That's why I came here uninvited."

"Maybe our Chief was letting you have a day to settle things back in Foster Town before he bothered you."

She cast a suspicious glance at me. "You one of them?"

"One of who?"

"One of them that thinks I'm nuts to be ready to fight for justice for my husband. My family says let the dust settle. Let them do their investigating."

"Oh no, not at all. I just told you I believe you're right, that it wasn't an accident. Is your family disagreeing?"

That seemed to mollify her, and she continued with a snort. "They always side with Freddie. Now they are all saying that he should fear for his life because someone is out to get him. That it was a case of mistaken identity. But it wasn't. I know 'cause Earl told me all about the mess Freddie is in. He knew alright."

"See there. It's a good thing you came today. This information will save a great deal of wasted police time. I'm sorry you have to be caught up in this. It must be difficult for you, but I'm sure our chief will be grateful for whatever help you can give him in solving this crime."

She nodded vigorously. "Oh, they will. Then the whole town will know the truth."

"Harmony residents want this crime solved. It means a lot to our reputation."

"I don't mean your town. I don't give a piece of doo-doo about Harmony's reputation. It's the fine folk of Foster Town that need to be enlightened. Freddie thought he could hide his sin. But he didn't bargain on me knowing."

She was on the edge of spilling the truth to me. Could I get it out of her before Jeff's interview concluded?

I put on my wisest look. In a somber tone, I said, "Sin is a heavy burden."

"Not for men like him. If you only knew what he's done. And been getting away with for years."

She stopped. Was our conversation over? I took a sip of my coffee, trying to not look nosy, but of course wanting her to continue. "You best be careful yourself if someone so dangerous and sinful did that to your Earl."

"Oh, he'll get his. When I'm done telling the Police Chief, he'll arrest him immediately."

I leaned conspiratorially. "Will he have enough proof to charge him? Or can you give him that, too?"

She instinctively moved forward and in a low voice said, "I think he suspected Earl was going to spill the beans. He was probably going to have to testify in court. But I knew when he asked Earl to golf for him, I knew late on Saturday. Trouble was brewing! Earl loved golf. God brought the devil in to tempt him. I begged him not to go."

She straightened back up. "I won't let this die. He will pay."

My seating position relative to Carleen allowed me to see Fred Foster leave the police station. And that was a good thing, because Carleen was expressing her exasperation with the delay in telling her complete story to the police. I needed to stall her for just a couple of minutes more.

"I feel your passion, Mrs. Foster," I said.

"You bet your britches I'm passionate. That's such a refined word. I'm pissed fits better. My first contact with Harmony's law enforcement came on a phone call. I'd just left the hospital room where Earl had died. Hospital gave me the message that the Chief of Police had called, so I phoned him back. He's all sorry about the mix-up. Mix-up? He called it something like you get two different size shoes in a box. Or creamy peanut butter instead of that crunchy stuff."

"How cold! I'm shocked he was confused about who was playing golf that day. But more shocked that Fred would let his cousin play to confuse everyone and then not have the gumption to own up to it right away. Did he even call or come to the hospital?"

Carleen growled through clenched teeth. "No."

"He didn't because of that family trouble? Oh no, ah, I mean legal trouble that the family wouldn't accept."

"You sure are a curious woman." With pinched eyes and a tilt of her head, Carleen spoke slowly. "Do you have some special interest in this case?"

Back off, Jackie. She's getting suspicious. Fred's driven away. You can let her go. But still I spoke. "Forgive me if I've pushed too hard. It's just that I have empathy for your situation. Family can be hurtful. Look, I'll let you be now. And I need to get to work."

Carleen stood. "I'll lay it all out for your Mr. Chief of Police. He needs to get some straightening out and hear the truth."

CHAPTER FIFTEEN

alking back to the studio, my thoughts wandered to other family tragedies I've seen. Granny Gunkel's daughter-in-law's greed tore her family apart and landed her in jail. Judy Hobbs went to extreme measures to protect her son and then had to prove his innocence.

And then there was my family. When I learned I had a half-sister whose identity had been kept from me all these years, I was angry at Aunt Ruth for being part of that deception. But stepping back from my hurt proved the best thing. Accepting that people must make hard decisions and live with them was a good lesson for me. Looking back, might they have decided differently? Who am I to judge? What would I have done in my father's shoes? He loved my mother and forgave her infidelity. In those days, her choice to leave Harmony to give birth and then give Carolyn up for adoption made the most sense in the situation in which she was placed. The fact that Carolyn's father desperately wanted to keep and raise her was dismissed. The discovery of my parents' secret and then finding my half-sister under her stage name of Beverly, along with her daughter Alli, changed my life and grew my family. I included them in my wedding plans by taking my bride dress search to Los Angeles, where they lived. The trip was fruitless as to finding a dress, but priceless as to spending time with them. I also confirmed one of my reasons for moving back to Harmony. That I no longer want to live in a big city. Never ever again. Visit…yes. Inhabit…no.

Beverly and Alli are going to be staying at the Whitlow Bed and Breakfast house for our December wedding. This thought warmed my heart. I cannot wait for them all to see how beautiful the village is during the Christmas season. Our Winter Wonderland planning group is growing bigger every year.

Scott waited for me at the studio. I gave him a quick kiss. "What a pleasant surprise!"

Mandy looked like the cartoon cat who swallowed the canary.

"What's going on?" I asked.

"Matt sent something over with Scott for us to see.

Right this way." She led us back to her framing room and there on the big wooden worktable were architectural drawings.

With a proud tone to his voice, Scott said, "Matt's been learning to operate AutoCad in order to do building plans for Drake Construction. I've taken the liberty of explaining some things we talked about doing to this space and he went with them to come up with preliminary drawings."

"And I snuck him in to take measurements when you went to LA," Mandy said with a wink.

When I inspected the oversized prints, I realized they were drawings of the future Parker Photography! My eyes tried to take in all the details Matt had put into these plans.

Scott came up behind me and gave me a hug. "You're awfully quiet, Jackie. We can change these. Matt can easily rearrange things more to your liking. But with these, we can get preliminary bids in before the final architectural plans are polished and stamped for permit submission."

Mandy watched my expression, waiting for my reaction too.

I was floored! And clapped my hands with delight. "I love it!" Hugging Scott and then Mandy in turn, I went back to the drawings. "It's better than I imagined. Takes my breath away!"

"Whew!" Mandy reached for her laptop and opened a file. "My sweetie just sent this over. Scott hasn't seen it yet either. Matt did a 3D rendering of the space. He said to tell you it's just the basic one, but he wanted you to have it."

"I knew he'd been playing with the 3D. Let me see," Scott said as he pulled the laptop over and we saw the renderings together.

"Wow! This is amazing," Scott said. "Look at this. If I may say so myself, I have a very talented son."

Scott pointed out the beautiful staircase that climbed to the second floor. It rose in sections, creating two landings. Matt added some potted plants and framed art to show how the staircase and its landings became part of the entire space instead of just one way to get from the first to the second floor.

"And I get to keep my balcony like I wanted. Look at the cute little bistro table he set up on it. Just what I'd imagined the other day!"

A twinge of emotion jolted me. I'd been expecting a sadness as this process proceeded because I'd be leaving the special little apartment Libby and I had enjoyed. I knew it was normal to feel this sense of loss, and now I embraced the life ahead of me. The man standing next to me was my new future, and Libby's too. After the wedding, she would come with me to Scott's home on the river bluff. She'd have a forest to run in, chasing squirrels to her heart's delight. Which reminded me I'd needed to talk Scott into getting one of those buried electronic fences for her. Wouldn't want her getting lost up on the bluff above the river. She's going to be as happy as me!

Mandy let out a squeal of delight as she saw the extra space created for her. "Seriously? That entire space is for my framing business? Now I'm speechless."

"It is," Scott said. "Jackie made sure we calculated the area into the square foot usage."

With moist eyes and a huge smile, she spoke. "Jackie, this is like a gift. Your encouragement and support are unbelievable. I'll gladly pay a lease for this space. My business is doing great, thanks to you. And now to have double the space is really going to allow me to grow."

Scott reached for my hand. "It might be a good time to tell her your thoughts, Jackie."

Scott had already made plans for Matt to take over Drake Construction. I hoped it would happen sooner rather than later, so Scott could take more time off for us to travel, go boating, and just enjoy life without thinking about daily problems on job sites and all the other headaches that come with owning a business. But what Scott meant I talk to Mandy about was something else.

I held up my finger. "Just a moment." I dialed up Matt on my video chat and when we connected, I told him how I appreciated his surprise of the architectural plans and the 3D renderings.

"And I have something I want to say, but to both of you because it will be a decision you will have to make together. Now that Scott and I are getting married, I've had some thoughts about my life ahead. With this expansion of Parker Photography will come more demands on my time. Aunt Ruth still loves coming in on Mondays and whenever else I need an extra hand. But she's comfortable financially and doesn't need the income. The perfect person to take over here would be Mandy. If you two agree to it, I'd like Mandy to buy into the business and become my partner. My asking price would be $1.00."

The gasp from Mandy, and seeing Matt's grin on my cellphone screen, gave me the answer. After virtual handshakes and plans to go out for a celebration dinner soon, we all said goodbye to my future stepson. The jingle of the front door called Mandy away to help a customer in front.

Scott said, "Looks like they like the idea. So do I. More time together for us. Have you heard any more about the shooting on Sunday? I read Stu's article about requesting photographs for any clues. Does that mean Jeff is stuck?"

"He might be unstuck after what happened this morning. Did you see the live broadcast by NBC? They were interviewing Carleen Foster on the village green this morning. You knew it was Earl, a cousin of Fred's who was the victim, didn't you?"

"I didn't see the broadcast, but the word got out fast that the wrong guy played that day. Quite a shock to hear that. He never let on that he wasn't Fred. So, if the shooting was accidental, it doesn't matter which guy it was, right?"

"But was it an accident? The world just saw the victim's wife on national television, saying it wasn't. I'm going to talk to Jeff as soon as he's done interviewing Carleen Foster. She's in his office now."

"Why are you getting involved? It scares me. Your curiosity has gotten you into dangerous situations before. I don't want to see that happening again."

"I know, but I'm a big girl, Scott. Jeff asked me to stall Carleen so she wouldn't run into her cousin-in-law Fred at the police station. He hinted I might get some information out of her because it would be a casual conversation, not an interrogation. I need to tell him what I discovered."

"Jackie, I'm not sure if this is anything important, but while you're talking with Jeff, mention that Angie Palmer, my golf partner, remarked on Fred having been involved in gambling. She said of course golfers are notorious for making bets on the game, putts and all that, but she hinted that Fred's gambling was different. Everyone bets in golf, but maybe not all at the same level."

Hmm, Mayor Fred and money seem to get tangled up. What Scott shared and Kim overheard at the party might be part of some bigger picture.

Was the shooting targeted?

Not at Earl, but at Fred?

CHAPTER SIXTEEN

*J*eff rested his elbows on his desk, rubbing his temples with small circular motions.

"Interesting morning?" I asked, taking the chair across from him.

"You could say that. Information is coming in fast and furious, but it's so tangled up I need to think it through. What can I do for you Jackie?"

"I wanted to touch base with you about my conversation with Carleen Foster over coffee..."

"Oh right. Thanks so much for doing that. It was quick thinking on Murph's part. She's quite a character, isn't she?"

"I agree with that. You should take time later to watch the interview with the reporter. They'll probably put it up on the station webpage. I think she agreed to talk to me because I said I didn't think it was an accident."

"Is that true?" Jeff asked.

"That's the way I'm leaning. But I'll still give the accidental shooting a twenty percent chance. Back to Carleen. She told me that Fred talked to Earl about covering for him at the tournament late on Saturday night. He said he didn't feel well."

Jeff pulled a notepad in front of him. "I might as well write down the points you are telling me and compare with what Fred and Carleen said at their interviews."

"She went on to say her family thinks she should let the dust settle and not stir things up. But she's fired up and said she knows Earl had the goods on Fred. Knew his sin and all about the mess he'd gotten himself into."

"Was she more specific as to what the mess she was referring to was?"

"She implied she had specific information, but didn't tell me. I didn't want to push her too much, but encouraged her to tell you everything. She claimed Fred set Earl up. In very colorful language she explained Fred tempted him with being able to enjoy playing in a big tournament."

"That agrees with what she told me. I wish Earl had let Junene know who he was."

"Carleen claimed that before he died, Earl told her he

tried, but there was so much confusion at the registration table. She figured it was a half try. Why bring it up? This was his chance to act the big guy. The semi famous golf professional. Earl had always looked up to Fred, so in his mind, for that one day at least, he'd be somebody. She said that Fred played on that angle all the time with Earl and with other people, too. She emphasized that now he was just a big fish in a shrinking, drying up pond."

"This seems to follow with what she told me," Jeff said. "She also hinted at a nefarious action by Fred."

"The fact that Fred fired the shot that killed his cousin?" I nodded. "She implied it. But then said she'd give you an earful of the truth. At least Carleen's truth. What did she tell you, Jeff?"

"She said that Fred's power and lifestyle were in danger of being exposed as being fraudulent by Earl. That he'd been cooking the town's books. Fred was at risk of it all falling apart and his house of cards coming crashing down. Her thoughts went to Fred doing it himself or hiring one of his cronies."

"Only she used more colorful words, right?" I asked.

"Right. She talked about Foster Town being run by Fred and Earl's family for generations. And now that family power was fading," Jeff said. "Again, I asked her directly what Fred did. Cooking the books is an old expression that people use when they don't know specifics. But she evaded answering by telling me she'd said enough. Now you do your job, she scolded me. My husband is dead. Arrest his murderer."

"Speaking of Fred, did he tell you he spoke to me yesterday?" I asked.

"He did. In fact, he took your advice to call me and that's how he ended up here this morning. What was your conversation with him?"

After telling Jeff what Fred had spoken about to Junene and me, I listened carefully as Jeff told me that Fred thought his life was being threatened. He'd become more fearful since he felt they meant the bullet for him. He put a unique spin on the narrative Carleen set up about Foster Town being a small town where gossip builds and sides are taken.

"And think about it Jackie, the only people who knew it wasn't Fred at the tournament were Earl and Carleen."

"Didn't his wife know?"

Jeff chuckled. "Listen to this angle. He says it was late at night and Doris, his wife, had gone out of town to visit her sick aunt."

"That would fit with what he told us. She doesn't pay attention to her phone and maybe that's why you couldn't get hold of her."

"Hold on. There's more. He says that she's been

cheating on him. That was only where she told him she was. I asked for the aunt's phone number to check it out. Fred tells me that Doris's lover could be the one who wanted him out of the picture."

"A little misdirection, you think?" I asked. "Look at that shiny object over there?"

Jeff rolled his eyes. "It struck me as a stretch, but I can't rule anything out. But wait. There's more. Fred also put another possibility on the table for me. Politics. He mentioned a couple of leads that I'm going to check into. I've got a feeling he's throwing up smoke screens to hide the truth."

Jeff flipped back a couple of pages in his notebook. "I took all the info he gave and there might be something here."

"That last part fits with what Kim overheard. Did Stu tell you about that conversation?"

"No, but Kim left a message. I haven't been able to call her back yet. Can you give me an idea of what I'm going to hear? Sometimes I lose my patience with that woman."

"I know what you mean. But Kim had some very helpful information in the past. This involves a conversation that she overheard at the party Saturday night. It was between Senator Bennett and Fred. The Senator was questioning Fred on how his legal case was going.

Stu did a little research and learned that he is under indictment for mishandling government funds."

"Wow, I didn't know that. What Carleen said might hold the most water. If he was afraid Earl had knowledge that could come out in court or a deposition, well, no telling what a man will do. And his alibi still needs verification."

"I have to agree with you," I said. "Somehow, she got a major news outlet to send out a reporter and cameraman. I don't think she'd have gone that far if she wasn't sure about Earl's death being a murder."

"Could have just been the old *if it bleeds it leads*. They are always looking for sensational click-bait news," Jeff said. "My head hurts with all this small-town intrigue. I'll be going to Foster Town tomorrow and do some snooping around. The county sheriff is their law enforcement officer. I'll talk with him on my drive there."

"Did you talk to any witnesses that were there on Sunday?"

"I spoke more with Doc, Earl's partner. He told me they talked about golf, and how the match was going, stuff like that. Earl had some complaints and laughs about getting old and slowing down. He let Doc call him Fred all day without correcting him. Doc would have left that day certain he'd played with someone who had been a small-time pro. The guy was a decent golfer."

"Scott told me something that his partner, Angie Palmer, talked to him about. She made a sort of offhand remark about Fred being a big gambler on golf. Might be nothing, but thought I'd pass it on to you."

Jeff made a quick note in his pad.

"How's the idea it was an errant bullet from target shooters coming?"

Jeff called Murph into the office to help answer my question.

"Well sir, last Thursday I spoke to the young men I'd caught up there before. I told them not to use the range on Sunday as the shooting would interfere with the golf. They agreed to that and wanted to watch the golf, so no problem. And they caught up with me shortly after the shooting happened, to prove it wasn't them. But there have been signs that others have discovered the place. I had set up a couple of extra motion activated cameras for that day, but nothing definitive showed on them either. If someone was up there, they must have used a different entrance to get in."

Jeff thanked Murph, then brought up how overwhelmed he was by the photographs coming over and all the other investigative work he had to do.

Even though I wished I could just say sure, I'll do

that, more and more, I didn't think photographs and videos would provide much detail or give any clues. "I thought Stu was sorting through those for you."

"He is, but he's sent over a whole batch of possibles. I sure could use someone who's familiar with photographic images to look those over."

Did he just wink? "Pretty broad hint there, Chief. But it seems like you could have one of your officers help with that. It's easy. And to be honest, Jeff, I don't know that there's a hurry."

"You might be right. But please think about it, Jackie. I'll be busy all day tomorrow. Could we meet up again later in the day tomorrow? I'd like to keep you in the loop if that's okay."

"I'm going to the Shady Pines Wednesday night potluck, but maybe after that."

"You could join Kay and I at the Stone Mill. I promised her a night out this week after her busy time with the golf tournament."

"Would it be alright if I sent Scott over there to meet you? You three could go ahead and eat. I'll join you for a beer afterward."

CHAPTER SEVENTEEN

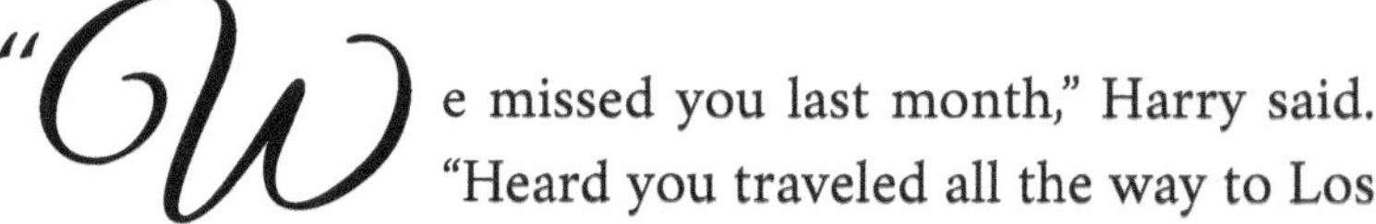

The Shady Pines retirement community was created from what had once been a Lutheran summer camp site. The expansive grounds spread up from the river and through a stand of huge pines. Evergreen needles carpeted the earth. They converted original camp cabins into cottages for the residents.

Parking at the community center, I grabbed my food contribution for the Wednesday night potluck and made my way inside. Elmer and Harry were just arriving and held the door for me.

"We missed you last month," Harry said. "Heard you traveled all the way to Los

Angeles to look at dresses. Seems like a long way to go for that."

Rolling his eyes at Harry, Elmer said, "Don't mind him. Glad to see you made it tonight."

"I'm happy to see you both too. Are the gals saving us a table?" I looked around the room and didn't see them. The gals were my way of lumping my Aunt Ruth and her buddies, Eleanor, Dorothy, and Betty, into one cohesive unit. That's often the way they moved together within their orbit.

"No, they are running late cause they wanted to make sure a new resident is attending. She bought the furthest cabin at the back edge of the property. But I'll grab a table while you put your dish out," Harry said. "Elmer brought our brownies again."

The guys were so cute. They bought brownies at the grocery store but always took them out of the store container and put them on a paper plate. I had to grin. I knew they weren't fooling anyone that they'd made them, but we all appreciated the gesture.

It had been a super busy Wednesday at the studio. The yummy odors made me realize I had eaten nothing since a small salad at lunch. At the edge of the large log room, near the stone fireplace, I saw Rocco and pointed him out to Harry. "Looks like Rocco saved a place for us."

Harry grumbled. "He always brings hummus and raw vegetables. What does he think we are here?"

"Quit your moaning," Elmer said. "He's a good guy and just cause he has unusual taste in food doesn't mean he's putting on airs. It's just called eating healthy."

Rocco represented a break in the gals' group. After years of visiting here from Chicago, he brought his boat into a dock at the marina for a summer. He ended up living on his boat for the season. Then, for the winter, rented an apartment. This year he had purchased a small home and had it remodeled, making him a proud and permanent resident of Harmony. But he didn't just move in on our village, he moved in on my aunt, to my delight.

"Jacqueline, I'm pleased to see you. I enjoyed watching you play on Sunday," Rocco said as I sat down next to him.

"Thank you. It was so much fun. Well, except not fun for the one player."

"I meant to speak to you about that. Do you have further information about that horrible incident?"

"Bits and pieces. I assume you've heard that it wasn't Fred Foster shot, but his cousin Earl."

"Yes, your Aunt Ruth told me about that twist in the story and I saw the televised interview of the man's wife from yesterday. She certainly had a colorful way of expressing her distress. Am I understanding correctly that she feels her husband was the intended target instead of this being a mistaken identity case?"

"Expressed distress is a kind way to put it. Carleen Foster is a feisty, fiery woman, but that doesn't mean she's wrong," I answered.

"Surely Chief Jeff will get it straightened out," Rocco replied.

"I agree with you, Rocco, in time everything will settle down. Hopefully by the time the course closes for the winter," Dorothy said as she joined us. "The others are right behind me. I mean what a fluke. I was in my beer cart on the thirteenth hole. I had my back to the hills when I saw the guy drop to his knees, then face plant right on the grass. Flat out."

"You were there? You could have been hit, yourself!" I said.

"Tell me about it. Luckily there weren't many spectators anymore. Most had shifted along to the final holes."

After dropping the brownies off and chatting with several other residents, Harry and Elmer wove their way across the room and to our table.

"Thanks for dropping off a copy of Carl Moreno's book to our library. It has a waiting list to check it out," Elmer said. "He sure was a great player."

"You're welcome, I hope you enjoyed it," I said. "I

haven't gotten a chance to read it myself yet, but then I don't follow golf so it's not that big of a treat for me."

Harry chimed in. "I watched him on television many times. But to see him play in person was a privilege. He's still got that powerful swing."

"And his short game didn't disappoint," Elmer said. "It was fun to read about his life outside of golf and see some of the personal photographs he included. The man's led a full life. He likes to ice fish and hunt, served in Vietnam, married an actress, did missionary work overseas."

"He's hot too," Betty said timidly as she and Eunice joined us.

"Why Betty! That's quite an observation. I didn't know you were attracted to athletes," I said with a wink.

Betty ducked her head.

"Don't be embarrassed," I said.

"Betty, you're usually not this vocal about men you find attractive," Harry said.

Betty blushed. "Guess I don't see many. Carl has that great hair, and he's so tan and fit."

"Ouch!" Elmer said, rubbing his bald head. "Would a toupee help?"

"Don't be such a knucklehead, Elmer. Carl is hot and you are not. No fake hair is going to change that."

"Eunice! Don't put words in my mouth," Betty said. "Elmer, you're a lovely man. And kind of cute too."

Eunice shivered. "Geez, way to lay it on thick. Here come's Ruth. Let's eat."

While the rest of our table left to peruse the buffet, I stayed behind with Rocco. The eyes of the woman entering with Ruth scanned back and forth across the room. Her alert, tense posture relaxed as she neared the table, as though her scan of the people here informed her that they presented no imminent danger. Rocco stood to greet Ruth and her guest.

"Jackie, please meet our newest resident, Sonja Bernardi. She just moved in a couple of weeks ago."

"How nice to meet you, Jackie, your aunt has told me so much about you."

"My pleasure. How did you luck into finding Shady Pines? It's a hidden gem," I said.

With a nod toward Rocco, Sonja said, "My dear friend told me about it. He's been keeping an eye out for a place to buy in this community. Months ago, he showed me photos of Shady Pines and when a cottage opened up, I jumped on it sight unseen. I have not been disappointed. It's just what I was looking for. Peace, quiet, natural beauty."

Eunice and gang soon returned, their plates heaped with food.

"This is going to be my undoing. I'll have to take out the seams in my clothes after a few months of eating all these goodies," Sonja said.

"Nonsense, Sonja. No more worrying about looking like one of your models. Let those seams out. Enjoy this good food."

"Sonja's a designer," Ruth said. "Rocco has told me that your work is beautiful. Are you going to continue dabbling in that here?"

My ears perked up. Might this be someone to do my wedding dress?

Sonja tensed, her eyes shifting toward Rocco. With his nod she spoke. "I've not included plans for designing or constructing garments after moving here."

Betty paused her potato salad-filled fork and said, "We have a quilting group here. You might like to join them."

Offering a weak smile, Sonja looked down at her hands and whispered, "Perhaps."

"Sonja's just settling in. Getting the lay of the land so to speak," Rocco said.

"Come on Sonja, let's go to the buffet and get some food before it's gone," Ruth said.

Once they'd left Rocco explained to me that Sonja and her husband were friends of his wife. "She's a private person. It'll take a while for her to get comfortable here."

"You saying we aren't the type of people she's comfortable with?" Harry asked in a challenging tone.

"Yeah. What's wrong with us?" Elmer added.

Eunice cackled, her belly shaking. "She may walk right out that door and keep going after seeing the likes of you two. Just take a look at the spaghetti sauce dripped down the front of your shirt, Elmer. And for Pete's sake, Harry, can't you ever wait to finish chewing before you spout off?"

CHAPTER EIGHTEEN

Once I arrived at the Stone Mill, I made a beeline for the bar to grab a cold Pulp Man Red Ale. Orin walked up to say hello as I waited for the drink.

"I haven't gotten to talk to you since Sunday. I heard about the golfer dying from his wound," Orin said, slowly shaking his head. "I see Jeff is waiting on the patio for you. How is his investigation going?"

"It's complicated by the fact that Jeff's not sure who the target was. Did you hear that Fred Foster never showed up to play but sent his lookalike cousin Earl instead?" I felt like I'd asked that question a thousand times, but it played a big part in solving the crime.

Orin nodded. "That does create a double investigative track. How did the national news reporter get wind of it so quickly?"

"Earl's wife did that. She's been making all sorts of outrageous sounding claims. Jeff is heading to Foster Town tomorrow to question the locals and try to get a lead on possible motives. That's the town where Fred's the mayor."

"Pretty impressive to have a town named after you," Orin said. "Say, was it even a murder? Haven't there been some issues with target shooting in the hills?"

"Murph's still checking out that angle. But Jeff has his doubts about it being accidental. Now on to something more fun, how'd you play that day?"

"Not bad. Shot a four over par."

"Hey, that's better than me!"

"But you won. Wasn't Carl your partner? He seemed like a nice guy."

"He is. And I'm sure his score pulled us up the charts."

The strings of light decorating the Stone Mill Brewery's patio were lit and the heat lamps warmed the outside area. No boats were pulled up to the dock tonight. The distinctive honking of a wedge of geese in flight overhead only added to the atmosphere of fall settling in.

Scott stood to give me a kiss before pulling out a

chair. "Sit down and visit awhile," he teased. "This is the first chance we've all had to get together since the tournament weekend. And now, I understand Jeff has the audacity to want to talk shop."

"I'll let you have a sip of your drink first," Jeff said with a wink.

Noticing their dinner plates had been cleared away, I told them how much I appreciated them waiting for me. "I'd promised Ruth I'd show up tonight. And those potlucks are fun."

"We're good here," Kay said. "But the guys' eyes were starting to glaze over when I told them I sure could use some help with the Winter Wonderland festival this year. We're making it bigger than ever. Scott seemed to think he'd be busy with wedding plans." She flexed her eyebrows and looked in Scott's direction.

"Uh, I didn't, uh…want to commit to helping Kay and leave you in a lurch, Jackie."

"Right. Sure." I laughed. "Kay, please let us know of anything we can do to help. But first let me backtrack. Did you tie up all the loose ends with the golf tournament? And was it a successful fundraiser?"

"It was an excellent fundraiser. I'm enjoying a few quiet days at the B&B before the weekend when I'm fully booked again."

"More golfers?" I asked.

"You know, I'm not sure. Could be. It's too early for fall color tourists. With all the publicity the tournament brought to town it might be what these weekend guests are planning."

"Did Carl enjoy himself while he was here?" Scott asked.

"I think he did. He left on Monday for a hunt in Montana," Kay said.

"He's hunting bighorn sheep out there," Scott said. I couldn't miss the envious tone in his voice.

Kay said, "I know hunting is a big deal around here, but I hate to think about someone killing animals for sport."

"I wish I could make a trip like that. How about we put it on our list, Jackie?"

"Sounds good to me, but I'll only hunt for animals with my camera. Maybe he's headed to the Glacier National Park area. I'd love to see that."

"You'll need a powerful lens to photograph the bighorn sheep in those mountains," Scott said. "I'll add Montana to our list."

"But our first trip is still our honeymoon in Florida, right?"

"You've got that right, my dear soon-to-be Mrs. Drake."

"Whoa. Slow down. I don't know about changing my

name. My entire professional career is built around it. And the studio's name? I'll have to think about it."

Scott looked crushed. "You won't take my last name? Jacqueline Drake has a good ring to it. Opinions from the peanut gallery are welcome."

Kay and Jeff both raised their palms, fending us off. "We are not getting into the middle of this. No way. No how," Jeff said. "But let's change the subject again. To my issue. Because I sure could use some help. Got some things done today and I have a few appointments set up for tomorrow. Hopefully what I learn there will provide valid leads for me. Point to someone wanting to see him gone," Jeff said.

"But which him?" Kay asked.

Jeff reached over to twine his fingers along Kay's hand resting on the table. "I don't know yet." Then sadly shaking his head he repeated, "I just don't know."

Kay could see Jeff's stress. She leaned against his shoulder. "I wish I could help somehow."

"I'll help where I can," I offered. "What about the research Stu Walters did?"

In explanation, Jeff said, "The crooked finances regarding Foster Town funds were discovered by Stu. He took it upon himself to start it right after the tournament and before we discovered it was Earl who was shot."

"What did Stu uncover?" Scott asked.

"That Mayor Fred had been using city funds to finance his lifestyle, modest as it is. He's under investigation and the allegations are serious. Foster Town's records have been requested and subpoenas are flying all over."

"And that was part of what Kim overheard too," I added.

"I've been handling other research done too, because one thing Carleen threw at me was that Fred was kicked out of professional golf years ago. Why was he kicked out?"

"Carleen told me that the expulsion from professional golf was over Fred's insatiable and illegal proclivity to bet on golf games. Before our 24-hour news and sports channels, it probably slipped quietly under the radar," I said.

Scott held up his finger. "Whoa, isn't that a big part of golf? Most all golfers have little side bets going."

"Speaking of gambling reminds me that you owe me a Wildwood fish fry from that game a couple of weeks ago, my dear," I said.

"How about I pay you back on that this Friday and we can let the kids treat us with the celebration dinner they talked about? I'll see if it's okay with Matt."

"Not a good fatherly example. Having your son pay

off your gambling debts," Kay said. "But now back to Fred."

"You're right, Scott, about gambling in golf," Jeff said. "There is betting, but not at the scale and in the manner Fred was doing it. And he wasn't alone. The whole story was hushed up so as not to bring attention to the underbelly of the profession. All the biggies decided to sacrifice Fred to save face. That's when he stepped into the life of a small-town mayor, but without a way to earn an income. He took on the mayor position and got to be a big fish again, only in a small pond. Now his shenanigans are being exposed."

"I heard Carleen in that televised interview. She was hinting that someone shot her husband on purpose. That he was the target. Or was I understanding that wrong?" Kay asked.

"You got it right. She thinks her husband was the intended target," Jeff said. "But I told her I must investigate all possibilities. One of them being that the shooter thought it was Fred Foster he aimed at. Carleen begrudgingly rattled off names of people with possible motives to kill Fred. She said she could go on, but in the end, she's still certain of the killer and that he knew it was Earl he was aiming at with the intent of killing."

I prompted him when he didn't tell us who Carleen accused. "I think I know who she meant, but want to share with Scott and Kay?" You could have heard the proverbial pin drop.

"Mayor Fred Foster." Jeff paused for effect, then began explaining why Carleen was sticking to her guns. "She claims Earl was a threat to the fiefdom Fred had built up after leaving golf. He knew Fred was taking advantage of the residents and his position in town. And she claimed Earl had a stack of proof of Fred's guilt. But when Fred dangled the chance to play in a big fancy tournament, well Earl couldn't resist. She told me she tried arguing with him not to do it. But apparently Fred's stint at professional golf put him in the legend category, at least with his cousin Earl. She claimed Freddie, as she calls him, knew just the thing that would put Earl off a few days. He knew Earl would jump on it. And voila...you have the perfect setup for Fred to take out Earl and eliminate one of the witnesses who could testify against him."

"So, Fred knew about Earl being subpoenaed?" I asked.

"I think he suspected it. When I interviewed him yesterday, before I spoke to Carleen, it wasn't in my mind, so I didn't ask about it." Jeff frowned, trying to keep timelines and interviews straight in his mind. "Carleen's story was that her Earl wasn't an innocent in the beginning. She admitted to that. She claimed that

Fred dragged Earl into things and back in the beginning it wasn't a big deal. So what if Earl made a couple of extra bucks once in a while? But then Fred got bolder and when Earl started saying no to him, she thought Fred became suspicious. His wife Doris tried asking her why the guys weren't close anymore. She was prying, like. Carleen asked her why she was asking and, as anyone who's met Carleen knows, she got a little mouthy. Told me she should have kept her mouth shut but Doris is just as uppity as Fred, what with the money he stole over the years. But that's neither here nor there now that Earl is dead."

"Fred claimed he was sick that day, right? Can he confirm his alibi?" I asked.

"No, he couldn't. He was home alone because his wife Doris was away with a sick aunt. I haven't connected with that aunt yet."

"Will you meet with Doris tomorrow?"

"That's the plan. I'll see what Doris has to contribute to this entire muddled situation. Since Fred is adamant the shot was intended for him, he also spewed out several likely suspects. Course it's nothing he did wrong. Oh no. These suspects are people who are jealous of him or have made false accusations against him."

"Like whom?" Scott asked.

"Like those humiliated by Fred. He said that people

think with his political power he can handle their mistakes. The local diner was recently shut down over a remodeling job that they didn't have a building permit for. The owners begged him to argue for them, but it was out of his hands. Then the couple who run a tattoo parlor and hair salon in a shared space had issues with the state Department of Safety and Professionals Services. They claimed someone was out to get them on trumped up violations. And Fred knew they figured it was him for some reason. He claimed the husband is part of a motorcycle gang and killing himwouldn't bother him one bit." Jeff blew out an exasperated sigh. "I have my work cut out for me tomorrow."

"I'll talk to Val tomorrow and see if she knows that salon owner. Maybe she's heard something through the grapevine. Listen Jeff, if you haven't talked with Kim yet about what she overheard the night of the welcome party at Harmony House, just hold off. I think I may have heard parts of the conversation too. Though Kim has a way of putting a unique spin on it."

"She has a way of doing that," Scott mumbled.

"It involved Fred and State Senator Bob Bennett. Let me talk to the senator first, but suffice to say it could validate someone looking to take out Fred Foster."

CHAPTER NINETEEN

My Thursday morning started in the usual way, taking Libby out for a short walk. Our Indian summer weather continued. I thought through how I would approach the senator with my questions. I had called Junene and learned he had golfed with Dermot, which was a good excuse for me to pop over for a coffee.

Dermot couldn't remember any remarks Senator Bennett had made about Fred one way or the other. No help there. I waved to Ginger as I walked by the Book Nook on my way back to the studio. She was taking down the window display of golfing books and it looked like a Dr. Seuss display was taking its place.

Dolly's Diner was packed. Breakfast was her busiest time of day. Val's salon was still dark, but it wouldn'tbe long before she showed up and switched on the lights. I made a mental note to talk to her later about the salon owner in Foster Town.

Todd opened up the studio today. I hoped he stayed on while the place was being remodeled. It would be closed for at least two months to complete the work. I didn't want him to head back to Chicago. He could still do his online work from here, if only that was enough income to pass the winter without working in the studio. I made a mental note to assure him he'd have a position with Parker Photography next spring. Hmm… maybe a promotion would be in order. I'd like to talk with Mandy about that as she'd be my official partner soon.

"Morning, Jackie. I need an opinion from you regarding what quantity of shipping materials I should order because it's a tight squeeze here now. Where will our supplies be stored during the renovation?"

"I'm renting a climate-controlled storage area for furnishings and I'm taking the photography inventory and computer equipment to Scott's house. But I want to be fully operational for the pre-Christmas sales period. I'm planning on doing a big sale over Thanksgiving and until we close the place up for Scott to get in here. I'll be clearing out of my apartment after the wedding, so he'll be starting in that area first. Make sure you're covered for that period of time. I'd say order more than you need because the storage area can handle it."

"It'll be amazing to see this transformation. This is so exciting for us."

This was a good point to talk to Todd about staying. "So that means you'll stick with us while the remodeling is going on? And won't make a beeline back to Chicago?"

Todd faked a sad pouty mouth. "Not unless you want to get rid of me. I'd like to make a suggestion to keep me busy and earning my keep during the months we're closed here. Why not keep the online store open? I mean why shut it down like you'd talked about? Maybe I could work out of my apartment as far as the computer end of it. And then manage the prints and shipping them by shuttling between the storage area and Scott's house?"

Why didn't I think of that? I swear sometimes my brain takes a vacation, or at least a day off! "That's a great idea. But wait, what about the framing component of it? Is there any way Mandy could find a space to keep that part up? Maybe run some data on the number of prints that are ordered with framing and let's talk about this later. Okay if I leave Libby here? I need to go up and make a phone call."

"Don't forget your calendar shows you have a hair

appointment in half an hour," Todd called after me as I headed upstairs.

I stopped on the staircase. Oh my gosh, I would have forgotten that. How did I miss that too? Aging? Too much on my mind? Now to remember to ask Val about the salon owner in Foster Town.

"Jackie, did you hear me?" Todd called out.

"I did, thanks for the reminder." As I was almost to the top of the staircase, I heard Todd again. "Oh, and Rocco called. He said he wanted to talk later. Something about the wedding."

My call to Senator Bennett went right through. His hearty voice boomed a good morning greeting. But after the pleasantries, when I told him what I was calling about his tone changed.

"Which conversation are you asking about? I talked with many people that night."

It was well known that our State Senator Bennett had his fingers on the pulse of the politics in Wisconsin. From infighting in the political parties to a mind ledger of political debts owed, and those that had been paid. When I told him the specific sentences I heard he exchanged with Mayor Fred, especially the one, *Just a warning, you're playing with the big boys now,* all I heard through the phone line was his heavy breathing.

"Care to share?" I said.

"I don't care to share with you, Ms. Parker. But if it becomes necessary, I'll talk with your Chief of Police. If I were you, I wouldn't think that someone had Mayor Foster murdered just because of his actions in the world of state politics, if that's what you're suggesting."

"Hey, old home week," Wanda said from her spot in the small waiting area of the Cut-n-Curl.

"I'm running a little behind," Val called out from her station. "Sorry. If you want, I can reschedule you."

"I'm good." I settled in next to Wanda after making a point of looking at the top of her head.

"Yes. I know. No need to make a spectacle of yourself. I'm here for my root touchup."

Lifting my eyebrows in mock shock, I said, "Me. Why would I look at the top of your head?" I tucked my own gray hair behind my ear.

"Just because you decided to go gray, doesn't mean we all can pull off the cruel things thrust upon us by nature. I will continue to have Val cover my gray roots as long as I can drive here and have the money to pay her," Wanda said. "And of course, as long as Val's still in business."

Val removed the pink cape from Kim's shoulders and

gave it a crisp snap. "To be honest, you regulars are what keep me going. I've stopped hoping that just the perfect fit of a stylist will walk in and ask to buy this business."

Kim's eyes were on her image in the mirror. With a few twists and dips of her head, she stood. "Perfect as always, Val. Don't ever leave us in the lurch. What would we do without you?"

"Come on over, Wanda, and park yourself in the chair." Val walked to the cash register to ring Kim up.

"Have you talked to Senator Bennett, Jackie? Was I right?" Kim asked as she reached into the depths of her oversized leather purse for her wallet.

"I did, and he confirmed what you said. So, I thank you for that."

Kim threw me a satisfied smile. "Glad I could help. Maybe there's something more I can add. You know how I've helped you before. So many memories! Trail cameras to drone video. We're kind of a team, Jackie, aren't we?"

"You're absolutely right, Kim. And trail cameras and drones might come into play here too. But Val, I have a question for you. Do you know of a beauty salon owner in Foster Town? Jeff received some information that she was under threat of being shut down by state inspectors. How does that process work?"

"Yeah, I know her. Got herself tangled up with a

tattoo guy. Depends on what the violation was. The state inspectors can be full of themselves and self-important. While some have common sense and consider the particular situation."

"I don't know what the specific violations were, but she's implying someone reported her and that's why the inspector even showed up."

"That could be true. Inspectors have a huge area to cover, so sometimes they focus on where they'll find a violation and can issue a fine. Means money for the state and a pat on the back for them. Plus, she's in a unique situation because of her husband's side gig. Tattoo parlors run by members of a motorcycle gang are suspect."

"Thanks. That helps. I'll pass the information on to Jeff. He's in Foster Town today looking into some things he's learned about both Earl and Fred Foster."

"If he's undercover, he'll stick out like a sore thumb walking into a small-town beauty salon," Kim said.

"I don't think he's undercover, Kim. But thanks for the advice."

"You're welcome." Kim took a moment to adjust a plaid scarf around her neck before reaching for her stylish khaki barn coat. "Anything to help."

CHAPTER TWENTY

It turned out that Dave did use his drone to film the tournament, but by the time Mandy contacted him about the call for photographic evidence, he'd already edited the video and turned the finished product over to the course management to use in promotional materials. "But you know me, I save all the data, so let me go through it again. Could you be more specific about what areas you want to see?"

As I explained where Chief Jeff thought the shot came from and which hole the shooting happened on, Dave also remembered the murders that happened there before the course was open. When he suggested checking for any video capturing the old access road Winford Carver had used to escape from the golf course, and the places where teenagers partied in the hills, I quickly agreed.

Murph was most familiar with the area where the shooter had secreted himself to get a shot. I decided to see if he had time to go with me and show me where the target shooting range was so I could see it for myself. He immediately agreed to take me there. As we drove the back roads, he pointed out the culvert recently laid in the ditch so the guys using the shooting range could drive directly in. The road in was barely two tire tracks.

Our first stop was at the rear service road to the golf course. Murph opened the lock on the metal gate blocking our access from the road. "The fire department has the code to get in for an emergency. They've allowed me to enter as part of the investigation into the unwelcome target shooters. The guys took a lot of effort to set up this range for both archery and guns. An uncle of one of them gave them permission to use the property. But as I've said, it appears it's being used by unwelcome shooters as well."

We drove in and up to a large metal storage shed. "The course uses this for groundskeeping equipment and for storing their golf carts off season. The resort also uses it to store equipment, tents, and tables used for events like weddings."

I noted security cameras mounted on the building.

Had these been looked at? I asked Murph to find out if the film from those cameras had been secured.

"I'll confirm that they can replay the video from Sunday for us," Murph said. "This comes out at the cart path on the course. I'll stop short of that. We can walk from here through the woods to the shooting range. The guys put up a barrier on their own entrance too. All because some people don't respect other's property."

We walked into the forest toward my right which, by my internal compass, should bring us to a point above the thirteenth hole. The forest was dense and filled with low scrubby brush. I couldn't imagine what I'd hoped to find.

Here, deep in the forest, I finally saw what was a substantial target range. Straw bales backed up paper targets. Life size animal figures with blank eyes were scattered between trees, their bodies riddled with holes. Plastic chairs and tree stumps surrounded a boulder edged fire pit.

"Can you take me to a high point where we can see the course? I need to get my bearings." As we made our way, I asked who else had access to the storage shed area besides employees of the course and resort.

"Like I mentioned, the fire department has access. But that's all I know of," Murph answered.

"Your own cameras were installed on the shooting range property but not along the service road. Correct?"

"That's right. And I didn't find anything incriminating on them."

"Someone could have parked on the service road before the gate and walked into this forest. To your knowledge is that gate usually kept locked? I noticed you left it open when we came in.

"Can't say, Jackie. Any time I've come here it's been locked. But I suppose it could be left open for people who might need access."

"Like whom?"

"The party planners, for one. They bring trucks up here to get at the setup equipment they need. The tents and tables. Stuff like that."

"And would they show up on the security cameras?"

"You're right! All the more reason to get our hands on the film. I'll get right on that today," Murph said.

CHAPTER TWENTY-ONE

Jeff slid into the booth across from me at Dolly's Diner. We'd agreed to meet here for an early supper when he got back from Foster Town.

"Sorry I'm late, it's been a busy but productive day," Jeff said.

Dolly appeared with a coffee pot and added to my cup. She hovered over Jeff's place setting until he nodded. "I suppose your delicious, barbecued ribs specials are all gone by now."

She reached over to fill his cup. "Jackie here requested I save one for you."

"Appreciate that, Dolly."

Jeff took a minute to pull out his cell phone and send

off a quick text, then looked up at me. "Ready for an information dump?"

"Should I take notes," I teased.

Jeff pulled out the small notepad he carried with him. "I have mine. But what I want from you, Jackie, is a big picture takeaway. I'm so mired in this case's details that I might be missing how things fit together. I need your help to put the jigsaw puzzle pieces into place."

"Without the benefit of a completed picture to look at," I said. "I used to love doing jigsaw puzzles. Aunt Ruth would find the corners and edges while I busied myself finding pieces for one object at a time."

"I haven't even found the edges and corners to this puzzle yet, Jackie."

Dolly brought out Jeff's rib dinner and my Cobb salad. I gave Jeff time to eat while I told him where Murph and I had gone this morning and that he was collecting the videos from the security cameras on the storage building. Plus, I shared the little information Val had given me about the salon owner. I also let Jeff know that Dave the Drone Dude was rechecking his videos.

Jeff cleaned his hands with the little wet wipe in the packet left on the table and rubbed his belly. "I needed that. Thanks for asking Murph to go out to that side of the course with you. We've been there, but it's always good to get new eyeballs on a scene."

"Now tell me about your day."

Jeff began by describing his interview with Doris Foster, Fred's wife. She started out claiming Earl was the intended target. Her reasoning was that only Fred and Carleen knew he was the man on the course that day. Fred was home sick. So that left Carleen.

"Did you confirm Fred's alibi yet?"

"Not at that point. I let Doris say whatever she wanted." Jeff held up his notebook, full of illegible writing "I tried to keep up with her in my notes, but the gist of it was that Carleen is either a good actress or a whacko."

I listened carefully as Jeff shared more of his interview with Doris. She informed him that Earl and Carleen's marriage was on the rocks. That it had reached a breaking point last week. But that Carleen would never let on. She pointed to the interview on Monday, and how it played perfectly into Carleen's hands. Jeff explained that Doris did a great imitation of Carleen pretending to be the devoted, loving wife for her sweet Earl.

"I agree that the drama I saw in that televised interview was pretty convincing. And I talked to Carleen at the bookstore while she waited to get in and see you. She was upset, but also very angry. Believable as a woman who just lost her husband and wanted justice done," I said. "But that might be the actress side. Did Doris say why the marriage was in such trouble?"

"Not at first, but of course I pressed her about it. She mumbled a few things. Nothing definitive. From local gossip she heard Carleen had filed divorce papers, but Earl wasn't signing them. What else was Carleen left to do?"

"But kill her husband?" I asked. "That's quite a leap."

"My thought exactly. Doris said Carleen wanted everyone to look away from her and toward Fred. So, she played up the grieving widow, which creates sympathy. Throw in that supposedly Earl had proof involving the legal trouble Fred was in…" Jeff raised his palms up and dropped his shoulders. "Fits the misdirection Doris talked about."

"Which would make sense in a way," I said. "But who to believe?"

"I knew I needed to keep an open mind. When I reminded Doris that the shot that struck Earl came from a long distance and asked if Carleen could have hired someone to kill Earl, Doris whips out her phone. She pulled up Facebook photos of Carleen deer hunting and told me she's been doing it with her family since she was twelve years old. She's a good shot. She didn't need to hire someone. When Carleen gets her dander up, she's capable of doing anything. Even murder."

"Whoa, okay. Do you believe her, Jeff?"

Jeff hesitated, rubbing the back of his neck. He rested his hands on the notebook before saying, "Do I? I didn't right in that moment. My hunch, my gut instinct, was that Doris was trying to mislead me too. Another big juicy misdirection. Just like she'd accused Carleen of doing."

"When did you bring up Doris' whereabouts on Sunday, since she was the alibi for her husband?"

"I didn't have to. She took it upon herself, probably because she sensed my doubts about her accusations regarding Carleen. And boy did she lay it on me," Jeff said. "She practically snarled at me saying I know that you don't believe I was at my aunt's. Fred told me how you were calling and couldn't get ahold of me or my aunt to verify where I was. She stood up like this." Jeff demonstrated the position Doris took. He stood, slammed his hands down on the table, and leaned aggressively toward me, our faces just inches apart. I pulled back to get away from him.

Dolly, passing by, reached an arm between us. "Stop it, Jeff! What on earth are you doing?"

With a deep intake of breath, Jeff sat back down. "Sorry. I was just reenacting a scene for Jackie."

"Well knock it off. You scared the bejesus out of me,"

Dolly said. "Now sit and I'll bring you a piece of apple pie to calm you down. Jackie, any for you?"

Catching my breath, I nodded. "Same for me. A la mode please."

CHAPTER TWENTY-TWO

"So where were we? Doris is hot under the collar and gets in your face. What does she tell you?"

Jeff laughed. "I reacted just like you and told her to calm down. She sat down but kept clenching and unclenching her fists. The story I eventually got out of her was that the aunt has dementia, and her live-in caregiver needed a couple of days off. She asked to see the phone number I'd been calling and said it was wrong. She informed me that it was the aunt's landline, not Doris' cell number. Then, cussing under her breath, she scribbled a number down and thrust it at me, saying this was the caregiver's phone number and told me she would verify that she was staying with Fred's aunt."

"And did you reach the caregiver?" I asked.

"Yep. Her story checks out. I also learned it's Fred's aunt, not Doris's. She told me he doesn't visit her often, unlike cousin Earl. He was a good nephew to her. Doris claimed Fred's waiting for the aunt to die because he's executor of her estate and figures he can get his hands on most of the stuff she had. Even get low ball estimates of her property value to divide among her beneficiaries so he's left with more."

"Hmm…sounds like Fred has issues with money on more than one level."

"Then I get this phone call from Carleen. Somehow, she knew I talked to Doris," Jeff said.

"Oh boy. Small-town phone tree."

"Something like that. Well, of course she's quick to add her two cents' worth by pointing back to Fred being the guilty party. Somehow, she must have figured out that Doris brought up her name. Carleen goes on about how Fred and Doris are in deep debt and about to lose their home farm because of his gambling and what he owes the syndicate. That's her term, but it's probably some small-time bookies who are after him. I didn't ask her about the divorce thing because I didn't want to stir her up more."

"Ugh…my head is spinning. I'm losing track here, Jeff. How about you break it down by the intended victim? First Fred. Oh wait, I forgot. Did you get to visit the salon owner?"

"Yes, I did. She seems cowed by her biker husband. He designed his tattoo parlor as a moveable operation, so he can shut it down quickly. She was surprised to see me, but totally understood why I was there, telling me that her husband has a big mouth, and he was pissed off, but she got him to chill. The inspector reduced the level of the violation and the fine when she explained things to him. Her words seemed legit. Did Val have anything to add?"

"Not really. Now back to who else would want to see Fred out of the picture. Might it be someone else from the family? Maybe involving the inheritance issue. Sounds like the aunt has some wealth."

"I have a couple of thoughts on that. And Doris only confirmed where she was and not Fred. So, he's still a suspect in shooting Earl. That would circle us back to Earl being the target. The only ones who knew it was Earl playing golf that day were Fred and Carleen."

"Now wait. Doris might have known too."

"Good point, Jackie. See, I knew talking this through would help. Maybe Doris and Fred conspired."

"That's a real possibility. But to what benefit? Why?"

"Money is often a motive," Jeff said. "And Mayor Fred loved money. One less person to divide the inheritance with? Maybe most everything Doris told me is really a setup. She might have been at the aunt's house, but could have slipped away and gotten rid of Earl."

Information overload for this old lady. So many moving pieces. Too many possibilities. We said our goodbyes with a promise from me to think about all we'd covered. That was the best I could do. I'll pull a Scarlet O'Hara and think about it tomorrow.

CHAPTER TWENTY-THREE

By walking the land with Murph yesterday, I thought it would clear up some things for me. Give me a feel for the place the shooter stood to do his dastardly deed. Had I accomplished that? After that talk with Jeff last night, I felt more confused than ever.

With all the criss-crossing of suspects and motives, I needed some concrete evidence.

My hopes that the shooter was caught on camera were dashed when Murph reported back that the security cameras from the storage shed didn't show any unusual activity. He explained that he'd checked the video two days before the tournament as well, in case someone had scouted out the spot ahead of time.

But now, the thought that the shooter could have

scouted out the area prompted me to text Dave. A sliver of hope remained.

Within minutes, Dave sent me a link to a video, explaining that he had done a practice run on Saturday. He was curious about the shooting range he'd heard about and took his drone on a brief side trip. From the air, the trees obscured most of the range, but he advised me he picked up a vehicle parked at the edge of the county road.

"You might want to see if Jeff can find out who that belongs to. It could simply be one of the guys with access to the range, but why park on the public road when they could drive in? Just a thought."

Well, it was something. From the video he sent, I could see the pickup. It was a black one, common for this area. From the air, a couple of features might help Jeff figure out who it belonged to. The bed of the truck looked like it had a cover. By the sun's reflection on it, it looked like one of the hard fiberglass kinds. This was unusual because it was impractical for farm use. Access to the bed was more difficult, and severe height restrictions limited cargo. There looked to be a sunroof, which was common. Not much to go on, but I forwarded a screenshot of the truck to Murph. He was most likely the one to help identify it if it belonged to any of the guys using the shooting range.

But it was Jeff who called me back. "Murph just showed me the truck. Don't know what the odds are, but that driver could be our guy. I'm going to have Stu put this out there on the online paper. Nothing to lose."

"With the line *a truck of interest*? Might be a dead end but worth a try. I'll print up some copies and post them on the bulletin board at Murphy's Coffee Shop."

"Who knows? This could be the break we need," Jeff said. "I'm going to give this to the county sheriff and ask if he recognizes it. It could be someone linked to Foster Town. And I'm specifically asking him to check out vehicles that our prime suspects have."

Todd quickly created a flier while I leaned over his shoulder to watch. Within minutes, I had a dozen printed copies to distribute around town.

By the time I made it to Murphy's Coffee, I'd already distributed half of them. Grace quickly pinned her copy up on the community board. Dermot came over to check it out and remarked that he seemed to remember seeing one like it over the weekend. The unusual bed cover stood out, and he commented it made for a nice-looking vehicle.

"If you can remember where you saw it, give Jeff a call. Say, how's Paddy doing with that Irish Pub?" Paddy Murphy, Dermot's brother and our former Chief of Police, was here in Harmony over the summer to visit his brother. Paddy had discovered that retirement in Florida was not what he'd expected. Too slow of a pace for him. When an amazing old building came up for sale, he used his savings to buy and remodel it. His dream was to have a gathering place for the community, like the Irish pubs he knew from his years back home in Ireland.

"That brother of mine. What was he thinkin'? I don't know. The missus is at her wit's end with the whole thing."

"Oh no. Have they gotten the pub open?"

"Supposed to but seems like there's always another hurdle is put in front of them. He wants to be up and running not only for the locals, but to catch the snowbirds."

"Snowbirds?"

Grace laughed at my puzzled expression. "The old, retired birds who pack up and head to warmer climates when winter hits here in the Midwest."

"Ah, got it! I told Paddy we'd come down to the Gulf and check out his new place when Scott and I head to Florida to visit his sister."

"He'll sure appreciate that. Maybe Sophia can give him some tips. She's sort of an event planner, right?" Grace asked.

"She is. I'll see if she and her husband Jack want to go

with us to see Paddy's place." Our honeymoon was only months away now. I'd picked up a couple of warm weather clothes during my unsuccessful bridal shopping trip in Los Angeles.

Then it hit me. My half-sister Beverly had hosted a party while I was there. She used a party planner who handled all the details. A charming young lady with rich copper colored hair. "Dermot, I met a party planner in Los Angeles named Katie Murphy. She was a charming young lady."

Dermot slapped his thigh. "Well, I'll be. That might be my niece! What a small world."

Grace agreed. "Katie is the daughter of Dermot and Paddy's brother. She is a delightful child and is good at what she does."

"I wish I could borrow someone like her for my wedding. I'm trying to keep it small, but with a move and a big remodeling happening within days of the event, I'm feeling a little overwhelmed."

Next door, Ginger was eager to let me know that she'd just tallied her figures from the weekend, and it was her biggest since she opened. "I'm going to have to do more book signings. The one your sister is doing in December will be another big one. *Becoming Beverly* has held a steady position high in the charts. I'll do a Christmas gift promotion along with it."

"I forgot she's doing that," I said. Yet another thing to add to the complication of the next few months. But grateful that Beverly offered to do the author signing here, as it would help Ginger's business. Her doing it while she was here for the wedding didn't involve me directly. Then why was I feeling this? Like it was another weight on my shoulder. Not enough walks and fresh air on the Mary-Go-Round trail with Libby. I was skipping my exercising.

"You don't look happy about it," Ginger said. "Is something wrong?"

Ginger's concerned look pulled me back out of my thoughts. "Oh gosh no, Ginger. I'm so glad she's doing it for you. It's just that I get anxious as I think about all I have coming up in the next few months."

"But it's all good, right? Please tell me you're not having second thoughts about marrying Scott!"

"Absolutely not! But this wedding planning is gaining a life of its own. I was just talking to Grace about it, and I discovered her niece is a party planner in Los Angeles. Beverly threw a party while I was there, and I met Katie Murphy."

"Love those small world minutes." Ginger clapped her hands in delight. "You should have a party planner like Katie."

"Nonsense. It's not going to be a big deal. The party

in Los Angeles was a birthday party for Beverly's agent. Katie did everything. Sent out invitations, hired the caterer, arranged for a florist and fresh flowers."

"So? Sounds like a good idea."

"For a small wedding in Harmony? I can see for the Hollywood crowd things are expected to be perfect. But I'm going for a small-town winter wedding celebration. And small-town parties don't have planners. Period."

"Why not?"

"Because, uh…well…" I couldn't come up with a good reason. Just that it didn't feel normal here.

"It's probably the extra cost for most people," Ginger said. "And since there isn't a big demand, there might not even be a planner in our area. Then there is the Midwest fear you might be perceived as uppity by not doing it yourself. And then…"

I burst out laughing. "Enough. You get it! Now, back to business. Could you put this in the window?"

Ginger had a twinkle in her eye as she took the flier from me. "Of course, I'd be happy to. Might agreeing to help with every murder investigation that happens in Harmony be part of the stress you're feeling?"

She could be right. I gave Ginger a thumbs up as I left the bookstore and watched her put the sign in the window. She smiled and waved goodbye.

Now on to Patti at the Village Hall. Oh, and I should

give one to Travis at the marina. There were so many places to post this. It seemed like a long shot. I texted Todd, asking him to send off a copy to the Hills Resort office and the Driftless Course for them to print up and post as well.

CHAPTER TWENTY-FOUR

I stopped in at the police station, hoping Jeff had good news and the truck belonged to one of the Foster Town families.

And he did!

"The sheriff knew of a black pickup with a cover over the bed. He just wasn't sure if it was one of those fancy fiberglass ones or a soft retractable one, but he was sending someone out to check. Should hear back later today."

"Unless they get wind of the hunt being on for that truck and decide to hide it."

"True. Way to bring me down," Jeff kidded. "Anything else going on with you, Jackie? You look tired."

"I'm looking forward to a nice dinner with Matt and

Mandy tonight. We're celebrating our new business partnership with a fish fry at the Wildwood."

"What partnership is that?"

"Mandy is going to be a partner with me at the studio. I'll be stepping back and letting her have a more active, hands-on role there. That will free me up to spend more time with my husband next year."

I liked the sound of that. But thinking about getting the legal papers drawn up for the formation of our partnership was just another thing on my to do list. After leaving the police station, I decided a nap was in order to rest for tonight's dinner.

But with Libby bouncing around and jumping up against my lap when I got home, I changed my mind, deciding instead to enjoy the entire walking trail loop around Harmony. Fresh air and sunshine would do as much for me as a nap would. Maybe a walk would clear my head enough to help me work out some more details about the wedding.

Libby was agreeable, so after donning a light jacket, we were off. Mary Bell established the Mary-Go-Round trail. She used her passion for hiking in nature to overcome the heartache she suffered, knowing her husband had fathered a child by another woman. Her burden was amplified by knowing she could never bear a child of her own. A sad history for this beautiful, well-loved trail. Judge Bell's illegitimate child was my half-sister, Caroline. A connection I'd only recently learned about. She took the stage name of Beverly Turner. Very few people knew that my mother's trip to Florida was to give birth and put the child up for adoption. My father and mother stayed together, as did Mary and Judge Bell. I'd come to terms with all that. I chose to be happy that I'd found my half-sister and her daughter Alli, instead of letting it bother me. Alli, who is well on her way to making her mark on the film world behind the camera. They both will be here in Harmony for my wedding in December.

Those thoughts prompted me to consider flower arrangements for our wedding reception, which led me to a decision. I took a moment to text Kate, owner of the Flower Girl. Did she think my idea would work? She said she'd do a little research, but the first thought that popped into her mind was that it sounded perfect.

Passing by the junction where a branch path led to the Harmony House, I considered some of the menu choices that I'd been getting from different caterers.

I'd been so lost in thought that it took Libby tugging at her leash to pull me out of my daydreaming. We were already at the Shady Pines property on their riverfront lawn. The gals and guys were gathered there, river watching as they liked to call this afternoon, pre-supper meeting. Libby knew well that Aunt Ruth would have a treat for her. She wasn't disappointed.

"Haven't seen you walking by in well over a week, Libby. You're lucky I still have a treat in my pocket," Ruth said.

"You're looking good, Jackie. All fresh faced and perky." This was an unusual compliment coming from the usually stodgy Harry. "Been feeling a bit of the brisk fall weather coming?"

"I have, sir. This walk was the alternative to a nap, and I think I made a wise decision." Seeing Ruth reminded me I forgot to return Rocco's call.

Ruth said not to worry, that Scott had invited them to the fish fry for later tonight and he could talk to me there. "It was so thoughtful of him to remember that I'd wanted to give Mandy my blessings on becoming a partner at Parker Photography. She's the perfect person to carry on our family business."

"That was sweet of him to think of you. Tonight will mean that much more to us with you there. But I'd better keep going. I still have to get home and clean up. See you there. Bye all!"

CHAPTER TWENTY-FIVE

They seated us at a table with one of the best views of the river that the Wildwood Supper Club offered. All of our congratulatory toasts and cheers were past, our plates were being cleared, and we had ordered desserts and coffees.

I'd learned that the reason Rocco called was to let me know that Sonja, his friend who'd just moved here, would love to help me with my wedding dress. He explained she was a very talented designer and creator of custom women's clothing.

"She appeared reticent to work on garments again. I don't want her to feel she's being pushed into something," I said. "Why did she put all that aside and move to an entirely unknown place? I mean, you're a nice guy and all, but doesn't she have family she'd want to move near to?"

"I appreciate what you're inquiring about, Jacqueline, but I am afraid I'm not privy to much of the direction my friend Sonja's life has taken. After my dear wife passed away, I lost touch with Sonja and her husband. It rather surprised me when she approached me about finding a pretty and quiet location to retire to. She's been through some difficulties recently and felt the need for a change of scenery, is how she put it. Her first reaction on Wednesday at the potluck was to not add any more pressure in her life."

"Which creating a wedding dress would do," I said. "I totally get that. I've been feeling stressed lately too. What with decisions on the remodeling, finalizing wedding plans, making honeymoon arrangements, taking care of packing for my move, and getting legal papers drawn up for this partnership."

Saying all that sounded harsh, even to my ears. "Please forgive me. That sounded terrible."

I turned to look at Mandy. "I have so very much to be grateful for. Knowing you will be my partner makes my heart soar. Getting through the legalities is just a hiccup in the scheme of things." Then I leaned over to give Scott a kiss. "And marrying you is a dream come true. You are my everything, but all this planning is my doing. I know you would have jumped at the chance to simply elope. So, I owe you a huge thank you for putting up with all those distracted moments when I'm worrying about this or that detail of the wedding."

"We understand, Jackie. We all love you and will try to help as much as we can," Mandy said.

"Of course, we will," Rocco added. "And please don't feel you have any obligation to use Sonja. But she sent along a portfolio of her work that she wanted me to show you." He handed me a leather portfolio. "She also asked me to tell you it would be a pleasure and an honor to design for such a woman as you, Jacqueline."

"She must have meant that you're so sweet," Mandy said. "Everyone can feel it."

Ruth spoke up, adding, "I want to take care of the dress since your mother and father aren't here to do it. I'll gladly pay Sonja's fees to create a special gown for such a special great-niece. And since she's practically next door, I can visit and watch the progress. I'd love to do that."

Then Scott took my hand. "I bet I know why she changed her mind. With your height and gorgeous body, anything she makes will look stunning on you."

"Geez Scott, laying it on a little thick, don't you think?" I said, causing laughter to break out around our table.

"Jackie, how can you say that? I'm a man madly in love with you, and I'll always be in awe of you." Scott gave me that cute little crooked grin of his. "And after all, we could move up the moving and get that off your mind."

"I figured those sickly sweet words were leading up to something, but no. I'll stay where I'm at until after the wedding. Matt, why don't you share some of the remodeling ideas you've drawn up? I'm sure Aunt Ruth and Rocco would love to see them."

Aunt Ruth's eyes lit up as Matt walked us all through what the new Parker Photography Studio and Gallery would look like once it reopened. He even pulled up the 3D renderings on his phone to show her. Rocco rested his arm behind her to look more closely at the phone in her hand. How very grateful I was for him to have come into Ruth's life.

My cell phone vibrated. I discreetly peeked at the text from Jeff. *Truck seen in Foster Town. Going there tmw.*

I responded...*Let me know what you find*

Will do

CHAPTER TWENTY-SIX

My first thought when I woke Saturday morning was that a new historical cozy mystery I'd ordered should be in at the Book Nook. Ginger must wonder how on earth I got to read everything I ordered. My to-be-read stack was building up. I was looking forward to the distraction, the escape, from all the other things racing around in my mind. Last night with my friends and family had been so relaxing. Hopefully, it was the beginning of a lazy weekend. Last weekend had been a whirl. The party at the Harmony Museum on Saturday followed by a busy Sunday. Then the awful news on Monday that not only was Fred Foster not the gunshot victim, but that his cousin was, and he had passed away.

I needed some me time. Escaping into the world of

1800s England sounded perfect, especially with today's dreary forecast. Blustery winds and cloud cover. Even with the poor weather, Libby was ready to go with me.

The coffee shop and store were bustling. Ginger's Saturday morning story hour was in full swing. The librarian side of her loved doing this. She was reading to the children while her new employee handled the cash register. I was paying for the book I'd ordered when Kim Walters greeted me.

"Isn't Ginger just the cutest? Look at her reading to those little ones. She's certainly holding their attention. Think her and Murph will get hitched and have babies? She'll be a terrific mother. Say, did Jeff find the owner of that pickup truck?"

"He's got a lead on one in Foster Town," I said.

"Good."

I took a gamble. If I said nothing more, she'd move on to a different subject. My escapist frame of mind didn't lend itself well to giving Kim a long update on how Jeff's investigation was going. But I did have a question for her about Saturday night, so I dove in. "He's still investigating other leads too. Like what you heard Senator Bennett saying to Fred on Saturday night."

"I'm glad it helped. Fred Foster withered under the remarks."

"Did anyone else hear him? I mean to verify what you reported?"

"Why would that be necessary? I heard it perfectly clearly. Are you suggesting I made it up?" Kim said. "My hearing is fine."

With my assurance that wasn't why I asked, and with a gentle nudge, Kim revealed who else was nearby and could have heard it. Then in her usual abrupt switch she was off and on to another topic. "I'm here to get another autographed *My Life on the Tour* book. Having that tournament in Harmony brought so many more eyes on our special piece of the world. Can you believe it? Yesterday I signed paperwork with a couple from the Twin Cities. They bought a condo at the Hills! Just like that. Oh, to have that kind of money," Kim said in a dreamy tone. But after a big sigh and shake of her shoulders, she said, "Anyway, I'm sending them a signed copy of Carl's book."

"I'm sorry, ma'am," the young gal behind the counter said. "We're all sold out."

"Seriously?" Kim said. "Are you getting more in soon?"

"Not that I know of. We sold out on Sunday morning. But I can ask Ginger when she's done with the reading circle."

"Well, good for her, I guess," Kim said. "Bad for me."

While Kim was distracted, I slipped away, retreating into the coffee shop area. I said hello to Grace, grabbed two coffees, and Libby got her treat. With Todd covering the studio today, I decided to take a cup to Scott, who would be in the marina readying his pontoon for winter storage.

The wind was definitely picking up. Between the book bag dangling from my elbow, juggling the two hot coffees in my hands, and Libby tugging me along, I almost ran into a man leaving the police station. The first thing I noticed were the tattoos on his muscular forearms. My next thought was why wasn't he wearing a jacket.

"Excuse me," I said, sidestepping to get out of his way.

He harrumphed something back at me as he climbed on a black Harley motorcycle parked at the curb and roared off.

CHAPTER TWENTY-SEVEN

y heartbeat quickened at the view of my fiancé straddling the side of the pontoon. He seemed to move in slow motion as he grabbed a pier post to pull himself up onto the dock. I stopped to admire the view. Libby did her what-is-going-on head tilt. My phone ringing interrupted my romantic mood. I reached into my pocket and dismissed the call without even seeing who it was. But Scott heard my distinctive ring tone and called out a hello.

"I was just enjoying the scenery," I teased.

"Really? You were? Want more?" Scott did a muscle man pose. "Like this?"

I pointed across the marina. "That's nice, but I was enjoying the way the wind is pushing up little whitecaps on the lake. Such amazing scenery is all around us." I held the coffee out toward him. "Brought you coffee. Thought you'd like to warm up on this blustery day."

"I know the truth, Jackie. You can't deny your attraction to my well-toned physique." Scott came toward me for his coffee and reached down to scratch behind Libby's ears. "Am I right, girl? What does she tell you? That she can't wait to marry that handsome Scott Drake? Or how lucky she is to have me? That she wants to move in with me today?"

Libby reacted, weaving in and out between Scott's legs. "See, Jackie? Libby's all for it." Scott grinned at me. "And so am I."

"I swear, Scott, if you don't stop all these pressure moves, I'll postpone the wedding until spring. I won't be bullied and coerced into living with…" My fake rant was cut off with a kiss and my voicemail tone sounding.

"Come on, old man. Let me help you get *Playing My Toon* out of the water. Sad to see the season ending."

"Not me. That means our wedding day is getting closer," Scott said.

"True. Well done. Spoken like a chastised fiancé."

"Thank you." Scott bowed and reached for the coffees. "How about I hold these while you pick up your message?"

The voicemail was from Jeff. It told me that the black pickup in Foster Town wasn't the one we were looking for. It had a soft, retractable bed cover. And he heard from Junene that she had noticed none at the golf event, but then she wasn't out in the parking lot all day. He ended the message saying just more dead ends.

Scott waited with our coffees on his dock storage locker. He sure picked a crummy day to take the pontoon in.

"It was Jeff letting me know he hasn't found the black pickup truck we've been looking for."

"What one is that?" Scott asked.

"You haven't seen the fliers we put up all over town?"

Scott shrugged. "Nope."

I described the situation of the drone video and what we were looking for.

"But whoever was in the truck probably had nothing to do with the murder of Earl Foster," Scott said.

"Or Fred. Remember, we don't even know the intended target yet. Fred or his lookalike cousin. Did I tell you about the wives both pointing fingers at each other?"

"Is anyone pointing a finger at the wives?" Scott asked.

I just shrugged. He had an idea there. Carleen hunted

local game, so she'd have access to guns. I don't know much about Doris. But right now, Scott was ready to pull the boat out and I stayed to help him hitch it up to his pickup. He would tow it to the Harris and Sons Marine storage building near the Stone Mill Brewery.

"Let's rent or charter a fishing boat when in Florida for our honeymoon," I said as Scott secured the pontoon on the trailer.

"Now I know why I love you," he said. "And I'll agree not to hunt while we're on our trip to Glacier National Park. It'll be strictly a sight-seeing trip."

"Your choice confirms that you're the right choice for me. Are you officially giving up hunting?" I asked with my fingers crossed.

"Sorry, but it's in my blood," Scott said. "The guys are planning a trip out to Colorado to hunt mule deer and I'm thinking of getting a new rifle." Scott slid his fingers across his phone screen, looking to show me something. He handed the phone to me.

"Take a gander at that high-powered beauty. Look at her sleek lines. Ooh…I melt looking at her telescopic sight."

"Should I be worried about competition?" He grinned as I handed the phone back to him. "So, you're going to shoot at an animal so far away that you need a scope that size? Doesn't sound fair."

"The wind velocity and direction will matter. The altitude too. There are sniper style skills involved."

"Hold on, can I see that again? Who sent this photo to you?"

CHAPTER TWENTY-EIGHT

With a screen shot of Scott's photo on my phone, I left and headed to the police station. But just outside the door, I stopped and took a deep breath to clear my head. I've just had a new piece of the puzzle dropped in my lap. Or is it really anything? Are you making too much of it? Knowing I do some of my best thinking while walking, I turned away from the station door, deciding instead to stroll our village green curving pathways. I needed to look at the big picture.

After fifteen minutes, I had a clearer plan on how to use this new information.

First stop, the Book Nook. Ginger was finished with her story hour. A small group of kids and parents remained, searching the children's section. A fire burned in the brick fireplace and created a warm comfy come-in-out-of-the-cold weather feeling. Ginger was able to confirm a couple of things I had questions about. My suspicions were right. She agreed to make the phone call I requested, but we couldn't do it on speakerphone because there was no private space. I didn't want any of this conversation overheard. But it didn't matter as the call went directly to voicemail. I heard the message she left and asked her to please let me know immediately if her call was returned.

Murph greeted me saying, "Hey Jackie, sure is getting wicked out there. Good thing we didn't have this weather for last weekend. I saw you almost run into Bear earlier. Don't want to cross that guy."

"Bear? You mean the tattooed guy? Is that his real name?"

"No, it's actually Irvin, but don't tell anyone I told you. He has a reputation to maintain. He's part of Jeff's investigation into the Earl Foster shooting case."

"Oh really. Good to hear Jeff is making some progress. Might I be able to talk with him about some more information I just received?"

From the hallway behind Murph's desk, Jeff shouted for me to come in. I found him with his hands steepled in front of his face. "I heard you saw Bear," he said. "Might as well tell you what I called him in for. He was the one who had the black pickup with the unique bedcover in Foster Town. Thinking the overhead photo might have been wrong about a hardcover, I went to the tattoo parlor and asked if it was his. Since they share the space, his wife was there and confirmed that her husband had such a truck, but he wasn't available to talk to me now. He was in Greensville, attending to some business. After explaining that I needed to ask a couple of questions, her body language told me she was hiding something. She called him and in no uncertain terms told him to get his butt over to the Harmony police station pronto. I'd barely gotten back here when he showed up."

Was my new hunch wrong? Could the whole thing point back to local conflicts? I was glad that Jeff spoke first. It might save me from embarrassing myself.

"He's not a suspect, but he gave up some very interesting information. Of course, I need to verify it, but there are a lot of fingers pointing in opposite directions in Foster Town. Want to hear what he had to say?"

"Sure, go ahead." I'd been perched on the edge of my seat, but now I slid back, ready to listen.

"Bear has a black truck like that but said he didn't park on some back road in Harmony last Saturday. He was on a motorcycle ride with his old lady and friends. He wanted me to know that we should look at Mayor Fred. What he said about him confirmed some facts

Carleen spoke of. He had been hitting up Bear and his wife for money to help clear up the fines for violations that the tattoo parlor and beauty salon were dealing with."

"So, was this just a shakedown or more proof that the mayor was in financial trouble?" I mused. "Maybe he killed Earl to inherit more money?"

"Or the other possible reason was that Earl had the goods on Fred and was threatening to expose him like Carleen said. Either way, I need to find out more about Fred Foster. Now what was it you came to tell me?"

Handing my phone over to Jeff, I said, "Take a look at this. Scott showed me this photograph of a rifle."

Jeff palmed the phone and zoomed in. "Pretty darn nice. And that's a serious scope."

"Notice anything else?"

"Not really."

"Zoom back out." I watched Jeff's countenance as the recognition of what he saw came over him. "Hold on. Is this…?"

"It is. The gun is on the back gate of the truck, but in the upper corner of the picture, you'll see the edge of the open bedcover."

"Who does this truck belong to?"

CHAPTER TWENTY-NINE

"Carl Moreno."

The expression on Jeff's face changed markedly from curiosity to incredulity. "But Jackie, what does it mean?"

Where to start? It was imperative that I lay this case out carefully. I started with a remark Carl made on Saturday night.

"Jeff, do you remember at the party on Saturday evening when you and Scott were on the patio talking with Carl?"

"I guess. Maybe. I talked to so many people that night."

"Carl said he'd been checking out the course and the back roads of Harmony after he finished with the book signing. It was so innocent sounding. He talked about nature taking his breath away," I said.

A light bulb went off for Jeff. His eyes brightened. "And the back roads are where this truck showed up on the drone video. Are you saying he was scoping out a place to shoot from?"

"No. Not then. He probably was enjoying the view of the course from the hills above. It is stunning. You look down at Harmony and the river beyond. But he might have used what he saw there that afternoon after a conversation he had with Fred Foster at the party Saturday night. Kim and I both heard it. You can talk to her, and she'll confirm it. At the time, I couldn't see who was speaking, but when their voices lowered and the tone of the conversation changed, it caught my attention. They were off to one side in the main entrance hall against the wall of the staircase and I was on the second floor near the landing. I couldn't see because they were out of my line of sight, but Kim later confirmed who'd been speaking."

"So...tell me more."

I had Jeff's total attention now. "As I said, I didn't know who was speaking until later, but it went something like this...

You got a few facts wrong old buddy.

Really like what?

Oh don't play innocent. We both know what happened. Only I got the raw end of the deal.

Don't threaten me.

Threat? That's a strange word coming from you.

"Now it's clear that Carl was warning Fred about something, and Fred implied that it wasn't the truth. I was called away just as a third person, who I later learned was Senator Bennett, interrupted the conversation going on between the two men. That's the conversation Kim had overheard and told Stu about. She confirmed to me that it was Carl who was with Fred when the Senator approached him and questioned his legal difficulties. Did he do it so Mayor Fred would get out of Carl Moreno's face? Most people held Carl in higher regard than Fred with all his issues."

I could see Jeff was back to being confused, so I broke it down for him. "Gambling cost Fred his career as a professional golfer. They banned him from playing on the professional tour. Certainly, he paid an enormous price and resented others who didn't suffer his same fate when they had done similar deeds. I read Carl's book, and he alluded to the housecleaning time. It was a wake-up call for the golfers. The gambling had gotten out of hand in the tour and Fred was one of the golfers who was kicked out. Carl escaped censure and cleaned up his ways."

"You're implying Fred hated Carl for the different positions they found themselves in later in life?"

I nodded. "Scott told me everyone gambles in golf but not at the same scale. Here's where I get to motive. I think Fred was going to expose Carl and the gambling he'd done. If Carl hadn't shown up here in Harmony for the pro-am tournament that Mayor Fred Foster, former pro golfer now a small-town mayor in deep financial and legal difficulty, was playing in too, we would not be talking about this. By coming to town and playing big shot author, at least in Fred's mind, Carl pulled the scab off an old wound and dumped salt in it. Fred spoke to Carl at the book signing on Saturday and an argument broke out there. Ginger saw it. She told me about the incident earlier today. Then came the confrontation on Saturday night at the party. Fred threatened to expose Carl's own gambling issues. Why? For money. Unless Carl coughed up some dough."

"Come on, Jackie, that seems like a reach. Just from a conversation at a party? So what if Carl gambled at golf years ago? You think being outed by Fred Foster about something that happened decades ago was really that big of a threat to Carl?"

"I do. Look at him. He's riding high in life now. Fred thought Carl would simply pay him to keep his mouth shut."

"But Carl was in the tournament. He couldn't have driven up there and fired that shot," Jeff said.

"Oh, but he could have. He and I finished second. We were in the event tent and he excused himself, saying he'd gotten a call from Ginger that she needed some more signed books. He had them in his truck and said that he'd run them over and then be right back. He didn't do that. Another thing I just confirmed with Ginger. Jeff, he left the course, shot at who he thought was Fred Foster and came back. The time frame fits perfectly."

Jeff snickered. "And he just happened to have a…"

"Yes. He had a precision rifle with a telescopic scope for his hunting in the mountains of Montana."

"…in the back of his truck." Jeff picked up my phone and looked at the photo again, slowly shaking his head.

"Carl Moreno wrote proudly of his time in Vietnam as a designated marksman in the army."

With a deep sigh, Jeff said, "A sniper."

CHAPTER THIRTY

Jeff mused. "We have ballistics on the bullet. If we could get our hands on his gun, we could prove it came from it. Do you have a phone number for Carl?"

"No, but Ginger does. I just asked her to call him to drop off some more signed books on his way back to his home in Tennessee."

"But I need to talk to him before then," Jeff said. "I hope you didn't tell her about your suspicions." He looked up behind me. "Look who showed up."

"She told me enough to agree to calling him. He returned my call just now and said he'd sign some and ship them before he goes into the wilds and will be out of touch for days." Ginger put a piece of paper down in front of Jeff. "This is his cell number and also the contact information for the hunting guide he is using."

"You should be able to reach him now, Jeff. If he leaves on the hunt, he'll probably be out of cell service range."

Jeff picked up his desk phone and dialed. Carl didn't answer, but Jeff left a message telling him it was imperative he return the call before he left for his hunt.

"Did he say when he'd be leaving for the mountains?" Jeff asked Ginger.

"He said not until early tomorrow. They had postponed the trip a day, so he'd probably have time to find a post office. He's in a small town, so if it doesn't work, he said he'd have his agent arrange for a shipment later."

Jeff picked up his phone again, this time to call the hunting guide. They spoke for just a moment. When Jeff hung up, he told us that the guide was sure Mr. Moreno was in his room and he gave me the hotel phone and his room number. "I'll give him some time to return my call before I go through the hotel. I'm getting a bad feeling. If he is guilty, he might think we're on to him."

"And if he's not, he'll return the call," I said.

Ginger fidgeted with the strap on her purse before speaking in a low voice. "He asked if there was anything else I wanted to ask him. His tone of voice gave me a chill. Like he knew something. I didn't know what to say. I stammered, and he just waited. Just as I began to speak, I heard the click of his hang up. I'm so sorry. I might have tipped him off that there was more to my call than to order books."

The loud ring of Jeff's cell phone made us all jump. "Oh hey, Kay. Give me just a second." Jeff covered the mouthpiece and told Ginger not to beat herself up because he had told Carl it was important he return his call too. Then he told me he'd call me later when he heard from Carl.

Ginger returned to the Book Nook. Libby and I went back to the studio, where I figured I'd catch up on some paperwork. Anything to distract myself from waiting for Jeff's call.

Later that evening, while Scott grilled our dinner out on his deck, and Libby was curled up at my feet, a text came through…

On my way to Montana. Will touch base with you in the morning. You were right yet again, my friend.

CHAPTER THIRTY-ONE

$\mathcal{S}$cott had placed our baked potatoes on the upper rack of the grill earlier while we enjoyed a glass of wine. From his deck, we could see down the bluff to the river below. Looking west, the river widened to form Lake Harmony. We have caught many beautiful sunsets from this spot.

Scott dropped two tenderloins on the grill and the sizzle tickled my ears. He put the foil packet containing asparagus, a couple of pats of butter and garlic pepper seasoning on before closing the lid and wrapping his arms around me. "Want me to get you a warmer coat?"

"No, I'm okay."

"Now please explain this. How in the heck did Jeff end up flying out to Montana? And what did you have to do with it?"

"It's kind of a long story. How about I pour us another wine and light the candles on the table inside while you finish up here? Then I promise I'll tell you how I'm involved after we enjoy all this culinary goodness."

During dinner, Scott told me that his sister Sophia had gone down to visit Paddy Murphy's new project on the panhandle of Florida. "She and Jack just fell in love with the structure and its potential. At one time, the town was a bustling port on the Gulf of Mexico. So, its buildings have lots of character. But, as with many places, when the shipping dried up, many of the buildings fell into ruin."

"Don't they keep a vacation cottage and a boat in that area? I think I remember hearing that."

"They aren't in that town, but nearby," Scott said. "We'll see their place on our honeymoon."

"Did I tell you I met Paddy and Dermot's niece, Katie Murphy, when I visited Beverly in Los Angeles? She's a party planner, sort of like Sophia, but on a smaller scale."

"That's cool. Small world. Now, since we're done with dinner, how about you share what you know about Jeff's trip to Montana?"

"How about we put on coats and go outside for a walk with Libby? The sky has cleared, and it's the full harvest moon tonight. We could pick up the trail along the bluff," I said. "The fresh fall air would feel good."

Turning right on the trail behind Scott's house took you down the bluff and toward the river where it meets up with the Mary-Go-Round Trail. But we went left to follow the edge of the bluff.

"The last piece of evidence that I took to Jeff today was the photograph of the gun you showed me. It was the pickup truck we'd been looking for."

"You were looking for Carl's truck? Why?"

It had crossed my mind that Scott had seen none of the fliers and posters we put up around town and that Stuart had posted on the Harmony Happenings online newspaper. Otherwise, he surely would have put it together with Carl's truck. But maybe not. Scott only had the photograph sent to him and might not have seen the truck. It surprised me that Ginger didn't notice it, or Kay. But I think we go through our days and just don't note such small things. Or he could have parked behind the Book Nook and around the corner from Kay's B&B. Whatever it was, Scott having that photograph was critical.

"We were looking for it, because it was a clue. Dave was practicing drone flying, as he was going to do some promotional video for the tournament and the course. Nothing out of the ordinary showed up on the day of the video, but thank goodness he reviewed the practice video he'd shot on Saturday. That's where we saw a pickup parked on the back road near the rear service entrance to the course. It just seemed out of place, so Dave flagged it for us."

"But why would Carl have anything at all to do with the shooting? I sure don't get it," Scott said.

"That's where a few other things that didn't seem of importance at the time suddenly took on new possibilities. An overheard conversation at the party Saturday night and what turned out to be a lie Carl told me on Sunday."

"Okay, so still, what motive would Carl Moreno have to shoot Earl Foster?"

"He thought the man he shot at, from the location he'd scouted on Saturday, was Fred Foster. We all did. Didn't you think it was Fred?"

Scott shrugged. "Yeah, I guess so. I mean, I'd never met the guy until seeing him at the party and then that guy on Sunday looked like him and answered to his name, so why wouldn't I?"

"That's just it. Jeff found out that Fred called his lookalike cousin late Saturday night to sub for him in the tournament. Fred talked to Carl at the bookstore and at the party and by how I'm seeing it, he threatened to expose Carl's own gambling issues back from a time when the PGA did what was called cleaning the house out."

Scott said he had a vague memory of that. It was quite a scandal in what was then considered a rich man's sport. What the everyman now enjoys, was once for the wealthy class. When they discovered professional golfers were indulging in the distasteful and unseemly acts of gambling on their games, it had to be stopped.

"And it caught Fred up on the wrong side of decisions the PGA board made, while Carl must have skated by any career ending actions," I said. "Did you read his book yet?"

"Not yet."

"I'll show you the section where he talks about that time, but doesn't mention his own participation in it. Plus, there's something else. Carl was a sniper in the Vietnam war. He disclosed that in the book as well."

"Boy oh boy, quite some detective work on your part, Jackie. But can any of this be proved?"

"Jeff must be certain it's Carl. He didn't fly all the way to Montana on a whim. The rifle and the bullet forensics should seal it. I've got a hunch that Jeff is afraid Carl might try to cross over into Canada. After all, the heat is on and he's only miles from the border now."

CHAPTER THIRTY-TWO

wo weeks later…

Baskets full of colorful mums, cornstalks tied with orange and yellow ribbons, and piles of pumpkins were displayed on the sidewalks in front of Main Street stores. The golf course was still open for play and the trees in the hills above it were turning on their own fall display. The notoriety of the thirteenth hole spread and golfers would blame missed shots on the bad luck that hung over it.

Word of Carl Moreno's arrest in Canada came ten days ago. His extradition back to Wisconsin was in the works. The broader golfing world absorbed the news in their own way and the arrest gave lots of fodder for gossips in Foster Town. Here in Harmony though, most residents were simply glad it was over.

Jeff had called me the Sunday morning after he'd arrived in Montana. In flight, he had contacted Canadian authorities of the possibility that a wanted man, Carl Moreno, might cross the border. He provided the license plate number on the black pickup and a photograph of Carl that Ginger gave him from her publicity for the author signing event. A border crossing guard at Chief Mountain Highway reported Mr. Moreno's crossing into Canada, but he could not be detained without an active arrest warrant. When an arrest warrant was issued the next day, the Royal Canadian Mounted Police apprehended him. Jeff subsequently submitted Carl's rifle for ballistics testing. It confirmed that the bullet that killed Earl came from Carl's hunting rifle.

As for me, I'd met with Sonja Bernardi, and she agreed to do my wedding attire. She was excited by the photograph I shared of a winter evening coat and looked forward to sketching ideas for my wedding dress. Kate came up with the perfect suggestions for floral arrangements. Patti Hunt knew of a farmer who had a sleigh and draft horses he hired out for special events. That sounded perfect! A horse-drawn sleigh carrying me across the snow! What a way to arrive at the Harmony mansion.

· · ·

The End

HOLIDAY HAVOC

SUZANNE BOLDEN

A PICTURE IS WORTH
A THOUSAND CLUES

A PARKER PHOTOGRAPHY
COZY MYSTERY

Holiday Havoc

Visit Harmony again for Jacqueline Parker's winter wedding!

With only days to go until Jackie's wedding, the unthinkable happens! Harmony's Winter Wonderland is in full swing and Christmas is fast approaching. The Parker Photography Studio is closing for remodeling. Jackie moves into Aunt Ruth's cottage to wait out the days until her wedding to Scott. The horse and sleigh are reserved to take Jackie to her wedding reception wearing the beautiful crimson velvet coat Sonja Bernardi created for her. **But murder shows up in an unexpected place, wreaking havoc on the best-laid plans!**

A Katie Murphy Cozy Mystery
POUR DECISIONS
IRISH PUB
beer
music
Wi-Fi
tonight
SUZANNE BOLDEN

ABOUT THE AUTHOR

Here are a few ways to reach me...I'd love to stay connected!

Please <u>sign up for my monthly newsletter</u>. I'll share things about my life...both personal as Brenda Felber and professionally as my pen name Suzanne Bolden.
Like/follow Suzanne on her Facebook page

If you follow me on these two, you'll be automatically notified when new releases are available.
Bookbub
<u>Amazon Author Central</u>

Check out my website <u>www.suzannebolden.com</u>

Thank you for reading my books. If you enjoyed them, a review is much appreciated!